HERON COVE

HERON COVE

Ruth Wallace-Brodeur

DUTTON CHILDREN'S BOOKS

DUTTON CHILDREN'S BOOKS
A division of Penguin Young Readers Group
Published by the Penguin Group
Penguin Group (USA) Inc., 375 Hudson Street, New York, New York 10014, U.S.A.
Penguin Group (Canada), 10 Alcorn Avenue, Toronto, Ontario, Canada
M4V 3B2 (a division of Pearson Penguin Canada Inc.)
Penguin Books Ltd, 80 Strand, London WC2R 0RL, England
Penguin Ireland, 25 St Stephen's Green, Dublin 2, Ireland (a division of Penguin Books Ltd)
Penguin Group (Australia), 250 Camberwell Road, Camberwell, Victoria 3124,
Australia (a division of Pearson Australia Group Pty Ltd)
Penguin Books India Pvt Ltd, 11 Community Centre, Panchsheel Park,
New Delhi - 110 017, India
Penguin Group (NZ), Cnr Airborne and Rosedale Roads, Albany, Auckland 1310,
New Zealand (a division of Pearson New Zealand Ltd)
Penguin Books (South Africa) (Pty) Ltd, 24 Sturdee Avenue, Rosebank,
Johannesburg 2196, South Africa
Penguin Books Ltd, Registered Offices: 80 Strand, London WC2R 0RL, England

CIP Data is available.

Published in the United States by Dutton Children's Books,
a division of Penguin Young Readers Group
345 Hudson Street, New York, New York 10014
www.penguin.com/youngreaders

Designed by Gloria Cheng

Printed in USA · First Edition
1 3 5 7 9 10 8 6 4 2
ISBN 0-525-47393-9

To Isabell and Frances Wallace
and to
Mary Annie DeWolfe, my grandmother,
with love

HERON COVE

*T*he letter came on a Saturday in May. Mama had just come in from setting out tomatoes in the garden. I thought it was rude the way she snatched the one piece of personal mail out of my hands before I could even see who it was from.

Her garden-stained fingers smudged the lavender envelope as she ripped it open. She read the letter through two whole times without a word to me, who was standing right there.

"It's a godsend!" she said after the second time through. "An absolute godsend!"

I concentrated on a JCPenney flyer. If she wanted me

to know what she was talking about, she could just come out with it.

When she finally looked at me, her eyes were starry with tears. "The herb institute," she said. "I can go."

She sounded like somebody had just given her a ticket to paradise.

"The herb institute?" I asked politely, when she started to read the letter again. Little stings of alarm were pricking down my middle.

"Yes. I didn't mention it before because I wasn't sure I could work it out. But here"— Mama waved the letter at me—"is the answer. Bea and Addie are inviting you to stay with them in Heron Cove for the six weeks I'll be in Vermont. They say they'd love to have you for the whole summer, though that might seem a bit long."

A bit long. I stared at Mama's watery blue eyes. They were always damp about something. She said it was one of the trials of being a sensitive person. Her short lashes glistened like pig bristles. They were the same no-color as her fine, straight hair.

I reassured myself every day that I didn't look like her. My eyes were hazel, dark enough sometimes to be mistaken for brown. My hair was dark, too, and curly. Unusual hair, everybody said, so thick it took more patience than Mama had to get a comb through it. She'd made an appointment when I was seven to get it cut short. When I jumped out of the chair and wouldn't let the hairdresser near me, Mama said, *fine,* but I'd have to take care of it myself. I liked to think it was my father's hair, though in the only picture we had of him he was bald.

"Don't stare at me like that, Sage." Mama pushed her wispy hair behind her ears as though she could tell what I was thinking. "This is a golden opportunity for you as well as for me. A summer in Heron Cove with Bea and Addie . . . it's idyllic."

I rewound the elastics holding my braids. "I have plans," I said. "Nina and I applied to be junior counselors at day camp, remember?"

Mama shook her head. "I don't know how you can even think of passing up a summer in Maine to be a junior counselor at day camp. Bea and Addie are absolute darlings, and that house, with the fields going down to the sea . . . If it weren't for the institute, I'd be there in a minute myself. It isn't all that far, you know."

That was really too much. I was twelve years old, and Mama had taken me to see my great-aunts Bea and Addie exactly once in my whole life. Even though they were our only relatives besides Gramma and Grampa and they invited us to visit every time they sent Christmas or birthday cards. We probably wouldn't have gone the time I was six if Gramma and Grampa hadn't taken us when they came east.

"Look." Mama handed me the letter. "It's written with a fountain pen. Don't you love it? I bet they don't have a ballpoint in the house." As though I would be as charmed as she about what kind of pen they used.

I didn't say another word. Not then. Mama swigged down some of the nettles tea she kept in the refrigerator and went back to the garden. I went up to my room and shut the door. I put my desk chair under the knob the way I did when I wanted to be completely away from her, which was more and more often.

It was the first time, though, that I knew she wanted to be away from me. When I was little, Mama hardly ever left me with a babysitter. She always said she'd rather be with me than with anybody.

Now the thought of getting rid of me made her cry with happiness.

I sat on my bed and read the letter. Bea and Addie hadn't exactly *invited* me. They said they had been delighted to get Mama's letter. They said they could think of no greater joy than for me to stay with them for as long as she could spare me, or I could stand them. Mama obviously had asked them to take care of me, and they were polite enough to act like she was doing them a favor.

I got up and looked out my back window. Mama was planting peppers now. She tucked them in like she was putting babies to bed. Her herb garden was twice as big as the vegetable one. I knew she was into herbs this year, but she hadn't said anything about any institute.

Mama taught in the nutrition program at the university extension service. She took the job because it worked well with my school hours and she could have the summers off. Every summer vacation, she came up with some new idea about what she really wanted to do with her life. She was fixated on what she called her personal essence. "Our work," she would say, "should be an expression of who we are."

I used to get excited about her plans. One summer I helped her cut out hundreds of gingham jar covers for the organic berry jams she was going to make. Another time we painted designs on the borders of the flowerpots and wastebaskets she planned to sell at craft fairs. Two years ago she was all interested in learning how to build houses out of hay bales, but then she thought maybe she'd start her own health-food catering business instead.

Now it was herbs. And Mama, who'd talk your ear off about her latest fad, had made all the arrangements to study them at some place in Vermont without one word to me.

*M*y mother moved to Hollins, Massachusetts, when she was expecting me. It's in the Berkshires, about as far away, Mama said, as she could get from her home in Spokane, Washington. She used to work summers at a girls' camp near here when she was going to NYU. She lived lots of places after that, but she decided the Berkshires was where she wanted to raise me. At first she got jobs writing grants and newsletters at home, then when I started school she got the job at the extension service.

We rented our house from old Mrs. Leonard, who lived next door. Mama didn't believe in owning something as big as a house, unless maybe it was made out of hay bales. It seemed like it was our own house, though, because Mrs. Leonard never came over or bothered us about things. The only time I saw her was when I brought her the rent check every month. I tried to stay back out of her reach, because she liked to pat my hair. I didn't want to seem unfriendly, but her hands felt like scritchy bird claws.

The Dorseys lived on the other side of us. I liked them a lot, but Mama thought they didn't approve of single mothers. I didn't know where she got that idea, when Mr. Dorsey helped her with things like storm windows and the car, and Mrs. Dorsey always waved and wanted to visit.

That's how Mama was, though. She might like someone for a while, but then she wouldn't like them as much, and would think they didn't really like her either. Mama just didn't like being around people as much as I did. Her only close friend was Nan Stanley. She and Mama had shared an apartment when they were going to NYU. I called her Aunt Nan, and her husband Uncle Hugo. I wasn't sure Mama would have stayed her friend either, if Aunt Nan didn't do all the calling up and making plans. We always went to their house in Pittsfield for Christmas dinner. Uncle Hugo used to dress up like Santa Claus for me. He and Aunt Nan probably liked giving me presents because they didn't have any children of their own.

I didn't see Uncle Hugo much, since Mama and Aunt Nan usually got together when he was out of town. He and Aunt Nan were important to me, though, because I didn't have any real aunts and uncles, other than Mama's aunts Bea and Addie, who were Grampa's sisters. My mother was an only child, and I didn't know about my father. I liked to pretend he was from a huge family and I had all kinds of relatives. I even named them. Some of the cousins were Luke and Emma, Robbie, Diane, Kathy, and Charles. Luke and Emma were my favorites. Nana, Aunt Jane, and Uncle Dan were my favorite adults, although I liked them all. Nana was much more like a real grandmother to me than my real live gramma was. I had a book full of stories and pictures I'd made about them. They all had dark, curly hair like mine. My real gramma didn't like my hair any better than Mama did. That was about all they agreed on, though. Mama and Gramma didn't get along.

The day the letter came, I went over to Nina's while Mama was still in the garden. Nina Swane had been my best friend since kindergarten.

Mr. Swane was on a ladder painting the porch trim. "Sage is all the rage," he said, just like he always did. "Grab a brush, young lady, and give me a hand."

"Hello, Mr. Swane." There wasn't much you could say to him, as he was always kidding. I knocked on the kitchen door and went in. Mrs. Swane was cutting coupons from the Saturday supplement at the dining-room table. When she smiled, her dimples made little circles that matched her hairdresser curls.

"Hello, precious," she said. I liked when she called me things like "precious," or "lamb," or "honey pot." "You're just in time. Nina's been trying to call you."

"Sage!" Nina thundered down the stairs. "Guess what! I saw Mr. Stotz downtown. He said he was so pleased we'd applied for junior counselors and to come in next week for more information. We even get paid! I thought it was just training, but we get two-fifty an hour!"

I flopped down on the living-room couch and began to trace a peach-colored rose in the upholstery pattern with my finger.

Nina stared at me through her bangs. "What's the matter?"

I shook my head. She sat down next to me and waited, shooting me little concerned looks.

"I'm not going to be here," I finally managed to say. "My mother's going to some herb institute. She's sending me to Maine."

"But we planned this forever!" Nina wailed. "Do you know how many kids applied?"

I just sat there tracing the rose.

Nina grabbed my hand. "You could stay here! Ma," she called, "could Sage stay with us this summer so we can do day camp?"

"Of course she can. We'd love to have her." Mrs. Swane answered so fast I knew she'd heard me mention the herb institute. I didn't normally say much about Mama's interests to the Swanes. Right then, though, I didn't care who thought she was weird.

"See?" Nina bounced next to me on the couch. "Ask her, Sage. No, it would be better if my mother asked. It's harder to say no to a grown-up."

I would have loved for it to be perfectly ordinary for Mrs. Swane to call up my mother. I'd always wished Mama would talk to other mothers on the phone or at school events, but she never made the slightest effort that I could see.

"She'd be mad at me if your mother called," I said. "I'll ask her, but don't get your hopes up."

"Call her now," Nina urged, handing me the telephone.

"She's in the garden," I said. "I've got to wait for the right time."

On my way home from Nina's, I practiced what I would say to Mama. I waited until supper time, when she was all excited about a weed she'd found behind the garage that was good for fixing poison ivy.

"Mama," I said, after I'd admired the weed and could get a word in about something else. "Nina saw Mr. Stotz downtown. He practically said we can have the junior-counselor jobs."

Mama put the weed in a bud vase and started to shred spinach for a salad. "It must feel good to be chosen," she said.

"Yes." I took a big breath. "I told Nina I wasn't going to be here, but Mrs. Swane said I could stay with them. Can I? Please?"

Mama, who considered her own interests so important, didn't think about mine for even one second. She snorted, right through her nose, just like a horse.

"Forget it, Sage," she said. "The Swanes have no idea what a fresh vegetable is, and you know their politics. Weekends are fine now and then, but never all summer. Believe me, that would not be in your best interest."

"*Your* best interest, you mean." I put down the knife I'd been slicing bread with and walked out of the kitchen. I managed to get my desk chair under the doorknob before I started crying.

The last weeks of school before vacation, my friends and I always spent lots of time talking about the great things we were going to do in the summer. This year, besides the job at day camp, I'd been planning to get my lifesaving certificate at the pool, and maybe try the ice-hockey school at Marin Arena. That would still leave plenty of time to read, draw, and do stuff with my friends. But after Mama's bombshell, I just sat there while my friends talked about everything I wanted to do and couldn't.

At home, Mama acted like everything was all hunky-dory. She either didn't notice or didn't care how bad I felt. She seemed to think taking Nina and me to the Dairy

Queen twice in one week would fix everything. Mama considered herself a very sensitive person, but I thought she was a lot more sensitive to herself than she was to anybody else.

If I had to go away, I thought it should be to Gramma and Grampa's in Spokane. At least I wouldn't feel dumped on them, since Grampa was always offering to send plane tickets. But Mama snorted at that idea, too.

"I'm not informing them of this institute," she said in the tight voice she got when she talked about her parents. "They'd think it was just one more of my fool schemes." Mama always talked like Gramma and Grampa were one person, which I didn't think was fair. Gramma was kind of hard to take, but I liked Grampa. Gramma was very negative about everything. She thought the world was going to ruin and had all kinds of horror stories to prove it. She talked on and on about nothing very interesting. Sometimes she asked me questions, like what did I want to be when I grew up, but she didn't listen to the answers. She took lots of pills for all the things wrong with her. She had them sorted in a round box with little dividers.

Mama didn't think the world was in good shape either, but she was always talking about things like the military-industrial complex, while Gramma was more interested in drugs and murders. Neither one wanted to hear what the other had to say. Grampa just wanted everybody to get along.

Grampa waited on Gramma hand and foot. Mama said Gramma wanted him all to herself. I wasn't sure what he thought about world affairs, because he never got a chance to say much, which was kind of like me with Mama. He was always very nice to me, though. Not that I saw him that much. They used to come for a week every other summer, but Gramma didn't feel up to it anymore. Mama and I went to Spokane once, for Grampa's retirement party from Grandfield Glass. Gramma bought me a scratchy lilac dress to wear. Mama said that visit was reason enough to never go again.

Grampa liked to make puzzles with me. He taught me how to tie different knots, and how to do cat's cradle and other string tricks. He held my hand when we went for walks, and he bought me ice-cream cones. But Mama said if he didn't speak up when Gramma held forth, it was the same as agreeing with her, which I didn't think he did. I could tell by the way he looked at his hands or out the window that he wasn't agreeing; he just wasn't any match for Gramma, or Mama either, in saying so. I knew he didn't agree with them about my hair, because he told me on one of our walks that he hoped I'd never cut it.

At the Dorseys' annual neighborhood picnic in June,

Mama invited everybody to pick what they wanted from our garden while we were gone. That's when I knew for absolutely certain sure she wasn't going to change her mind about me going to Maine.

The last day of school was June 22. I always went with the Swanes to their camp on Otis Lake the weekend after school let out. This year, Mama said I couldn't go because we had to get my clothes ready. I was leaving for Heron Cove on the twenty-sixth. I was going on a bus.

"I thought your mom's program didn't start until July," Nina said when I told her.

"It doesn't. And I figured she would drive me to Heron Cove and stay to visit a little with her aunts, since she's so crazy about them all of a sudden."

Nina reached over and patted my hand. We were sitting on her front steps. "I'll write to you," she said. "I'll write every day. Maybe Heron Cove won't be so bad. It has a nice name." She jumped up and went into the house. When she came back, she had some safety pins and the painted box she kept beads in.

"Let's make new friendship pins," she said. We picked out the smallest beads and threaded them onto the pins. I fastened the two she made to the tops of my sneaker laces, and she put the ones I made on hers. To make up for the weekend at Otis Lake, her parents took us to the carnival in Amherst that night.

Mama went over the bus schedule with me the day before I left. I paid attention even though I didn't want to, because I was nervous about it. I had to change buses in Boston. What if I didn't get off in time? What if I got on the wrong bus?

"I think you'll enjoy the ride," Mama said when she finished showing me how to read the schedule of stops. "You'll be up higher and able to see better than in the car. I'd drive you myself, but there's no telling how many miles are left in Persephone." Mama didn't even have a normal name for her car.

"It does take a bit longer," she said when I didn't answer. For the first time, she sounded a little uncertain. According to the schedule, I would be alone on a bus for twelve hours going somewhere I didn't want to go. That was almost twice as long as it would take in the car.

The next morning I couldn't eat the oatmeal Mama fixed. That got to her, though by then I'd stopped trying to let her know how much I didn't want to go.

"You have to have nourishment for the long day that's ahead of you." She sounded as if she might cry. Not because I was leaving, but because I didn't have enough food in me.

The bus pulled up to Daggett's Pharmacy right on time.

"That's a good sign," Mama said. She was back to being perky. She hugged and kissed me, and nuzzled her nose on my cheek the way she used to when I was little.

I sat up front. I took out the red bandanna I'd brought and spread it carefully across the back of the seat where my hair touched. Mrs. Swane had told me about someone who got lice from a headrest on public transportation. I'd left my hair loose for courage, so I checked several times to make sure the bandanna covered the whole area.

I put my backpack in the overhead rack, then I took it down and put it between my feet. I tried not to look out the window, but I did notice Mama talking to the bus driver. She was still there when the door sighed shut, the brakes hissed free, and we roared slowly away.

We turned the corner at Lenny's Shoes, went past Berkshire Books, past Sal's Pizza, past the Mobil station that marked the end of Hollins and the beginning of the highway to the Massachusetts Turnpike. I watched it all, my face square to the window, as though I'd never seen it before. I'd learned in kindergarten that the trick to not crying was to keep your eyelids up.

Don't sit here! I silently ordered any man who got on at the bus stops. I was a little nervous about men I didn't know.

A woman dragged down with shopping bags got on in Springfield. "Excuse me, honey," she said as she jammed two of them in against my legs. A box wrapped in Mickey Mouse paper fell out of a bag she tried to fit in the overhead rack. "Excuse me," she said again when she sank down next to me. She put on glasses, took out a book, and opened it to a pink, crocheted marker. By the time we were back on the turnpike, her head was jerking forward and she was snoring.

I felt better with the woman next to me. I wound my finger around and around a piece of my hair until I fell asleep, too.

I woke up in a panic. Where were we? Had I missed my stop?

"We're coming into Boston," the woman next to me said. "It'll be a few minutes yet." She stood up and yanked her overhead bags down, then sat bolt upright clutching the string handles as we lurched through streets that looked too narrow and full of traffic for us to fit.

"Your bus leaves Gate Four in thirty-five minutes," the driver said when he helped me down the steps. "I'll be sure your bag gets on it."

"Thank you," I said. I didn't want to leave him, but I followed the other passengers into the terminal. A young woman with a little boy on a wrist leash met the woman who'd sat next to me. She had too much stuff of her own to help with all the shopping bags.

I found Gate Four, then I used the restroom. I was

careful not to touch the seat. I got peanut-butter crackers, orange soda, and a Charleston Chew from the vending machines. I sat as close as I could to the gate and ate the stuff I'd bought instead of the bean sandwich Mama had made.

I tried not to stare at a teenage girl who was doing some kind of private dance near the vending machines. One side of her head was shaved. The other side had maroon-colored hair that looked stiff as a board. She had pink-and-green striped socks and purple high-top sneakers. I really liked the sneakers.

When she finished her dance, the girl came and sat down next to me.

"Hi, kid," she said. "Where you going?"

I hesitated. I'd heard stories about urban youth and about bus stations. Then I said, "To Maine."

The girl nodded. "Me, too." I thought she might have decided that just then until I saw a ticket sticking out of her tank top.

"See ya." She danced off and I sat back to wait, keeping my eyes glued to the door at Gate Four for any sign of action.

The girl with half her hair
followed me onto the bus and into a seat as though we'd
agreed to travel together.

"Whatta ya doing?" she asked when I spread my red
bandanna across the back of the seat.

"Lice," I said. "I know someone who got them from
a headrest."

"Gross." The girl rummaged through her backpack
and hauled out a crumpled napkin. She smoothed it behind her own head. I liked the way she took my word
for it. She turned her attention to her Discman, but as
soon as we were out of the city streets, she took off her
earphones and turned to me.

"My name's Miriam," she said. "I'm going up to Bar Harbor to look for a job. What about you?"

"My name is Sage," I said. "I get off in Ellsworth. I'm spending six weeks with my great-aunts in Heron Cove."

"That's different," Miriam said. "Most kids get sent to summer camp. You like these great-aunts?"

"I only met them once," I said. "I liked them then. They're twins."

"No way! I don't think of twins as being old. Do they look alike?"

Miriam's interest surprised me. "No, they don't look anything alike," I said. I remembered I almost cried when I first saw Bea and Addie. I thought twins were the greatest thing, but they didn't even look like sisters, though Bea and Grampa looked a little alike. As soon as they spoke to me, it had been all right. Mama had been reminding me of how we'd taken to one another. That was when I was six, though. Lots of people liked little kids. Big ones were an entirely different matter, as Mama herself said often enough.

"Do their names rhyme?" Miriam asked. "Like Dell and Nell? Or Polly and Molly?"

I shook my head. "Their names are Bea and Addie."

"Bea and Addie." Miriam thought that over. "They sound nice," she decided. She studied me. "Why did your mother name you Sage?"

I told her. What I never told anybody, not even Nina. "She was into Native American rituals when I was born. She burned sage to purify the first air I would breathe, then she gave me the name to continue the blessing."

"Cool." The way Miriam said that made me feel almost proud my mother was different. And then she asked, "What about your father? Was he into the Native American stuff, too?"

I scratched at a spot on my cuff. Sooner or later, everyone wanted to know about my father. "I guess so," I said. "They met at a seminar on Native American literature." After a moment I added, "He never lived with us."

"You're lucky there," Miriam said. "My father did." She tipped her seat back and closed her eyes.

I lay back, too, and wondered what kind of father you'd be better without. I was certain my father wasn't like that. His name was Robert Kastenberg. I could have been Sage Kastenberg, instead of Sage Miller. Sometimes I signed my name that way. Sage Kastenberg. It was a big difference between Mama and me, that half of me was from a family she was not related to and knew nothing about.

I had our only picture of my father wrapped in a Kleenex in my duffel. Mama would never miss it. She hadn't said anything when I took it out of the photo album and put it in a corner of my mirror last winter. It wasn't a very good picture. It was at a distance and a little overexposed. Sun reflected off his dark-rimmed glasses, so I couldn't see his eyes. I could tell he was tall and thin. I thought his mouth looked wide like mine. He was smiling. I liked how he was standing with his hands on his hips and his feet apart. His collar was open and his sleeves were rolled up. He looked like the kind of man you could talk to. Which I did. All the time. Back at the bus station, I'd been telling him how nervous I was that I'd get on the wrong bus.

Mama said she'd told me all she knew about him. He was a geologist. He was from Toronto, which meant I was half Canadian, and he traveled a lot. He was older than she was. He'd just gotten divorced when they met at the seminar. "I loved him," Mama had said, "and then I didn't. He turned out to be the father of the child I wanted and was afraid I'd never have. I'm eternally grateful." As simple as that. She saw him two times after the seminar and never told him about me.

I shot my seat upright and began playing an old alphabet game with the highway signs. *A* my name is Alice, *B* my name is Bob. But I could still hear my mother saying in her matter-of-fact way, "I loved him, and then I didn't."

*W*hen Miriam woke up, we played gin and hangman. We talked about teachers and favorite books and soap operas. Mama and I didn't have a TV, but I knew some of the soaps from watching at Nina's.

"Are you nervous?" Miriam asked as the bus got near Ellsworth. She examined her hair and face, even her teeth, in a green-enameled pocket mirror. "I'll get off with you and check, just to make sure everything's okay."

Addie was right by the steps when the bus door opened. I'd been worried I wouldn't recognize my great-aunts, but as soon as I saw her, I knew it was Addie. She was shorter and sturdier than Bea, and more talkative. She looked like she was expecting a big treat.

"Right on time!" she cheered. She kissed me loudly on my cheek and thumped my back. "I remember that hair. Wait till Bea gets a look at you!" She noticed Miriam giving her the once-over. "Hello, dear, are you coming with us, too?"

"I wish!" Miriam gave me the thumbs-up sign. "Take care, kid," she said, and got back on the bus.

"How nice you had someone to talk to," Addie said as we stuffed my duffel into the trunk of her old brown-and-white Plymouth. "I met one of my dearest friends years ago on a bus from Chicago to Boston."

When we were in the car, she locked the doors, checked the seat belts and the car mirrors, then took off so fast the tires screeched.

"Such a long trip for you," she said, "and such a long way yet to go." She pressed the accelerator even more firmly. "We'll catch a bite to eat and be home by dark."

"I'm sorry you had to come this far." I stared at the rushing landscape, embarrassed all over again at what Mama had asked of her aunts.

"I've had the car gassed and ready for a week. I tell you, dear, we've been like two kids before Christmas. Bea wanted to come, but it was our turn to host the book discussion group. It always meets at four the last Monday of the month. We drew straws and she lost." Addie looked so pleased with herself that I smiled. Still, I wasn't going to let Mama off the hook. The fact her aunts were so nice about taking care of me didn't mean it was okay for her to ignore them until she needed a favor.

We got to Heron Cove at last light. "Here we are!" Addie announced as we came out of a dark tunnel of trees and turned into the drive by the gabled white house. The kitchen door opened, the screen banged, and Bea came across the grass. She was several inches taller than me, and I was already five-six. She bent to kiss my cheek, soft as a butterfly, and said, "Come right in. Let Addie get the bags."

I smiled at her, then stood still as the fragrance of the air hit me. I remembered that smell. A mixture of wild roses, meadow grass, and the sea. The remembering stirred an ache in my chest. I busied myself with my stuff, but the ache squeezed tighter when I stepped into the kitchen.

Everything was as it had been. The wooden table by the window, the door into the pantry, the drying rack over the stove. When I was six I'd loved working the pulley to raise and lower that rack.

The dining room had the same dark wood cabinet

with glass doors, the same glittering prisms in the light over the table. African violets still lined the bay window in the parlor, the piano stool waited to be spun to the right height. I remembered the creak of the stairs, the carved spindles, the polished banister. At the top I turned toward the room I'd shared with Mama.

"You'll be in here, dear," Addie said. She switched on a lamp in a room at the back. "The bathroom is first door down the hall there. You get yourself settled a bit, then come join us in the kitchen. We always have a little something to eat before we turn in."

It was a shock, everything being so familiar. I hadn't known I remembered it all so well. I sat in the white rocker and looked around me until the surprising tightness in my throat and chest eased. Bea had made the bright quilt on the bed, Addie had made the braid rug. Something else I seemed to know from that long-ago visit. The tall double windows looked across the field to the sea. In the lamplight the worn wood of the bed, the table next to it, and the dresser gleamed smooth as dark honey.

I unpacked my duffel into the dresser drawers, put my pajamas on the bed, and went down to the kitchen. Both Bea and Addie came right up to me and stared into my eyes.

"As I thought," Addie said.

"Without a doubt." Bea nodded. They stepped back and smiled at me. "Your eyes," Bea said gently. "They're hazel. McClure eyes."

"They're the one thing Bea and I have in common," Addie said. "Our mother had them, too. And she had dark brows just like yours. Yours have darkened since you were a tyke. It was quite a jolt, seeing how you resemble her."

"A most pleasant one," Bea assured me. "We thought the world of our mother and her family. Of course, her mother was a Bond before she married Grandfather Mc-Clure. All fine people. Our grandmother and grandfather McClure built this house in 1886, three years before Mother was born. Addie and I were raised here after Mother died."

"Don't get started, Bea. The poor child's exhausted." Addie sliced oatmeal bread. It was chewy and sweet. I ate two slices with butter and a glass of milk.

Bea had a book all picked out for my bedtime reading. "It's about Wilfred Grenfell's mission to the arctic communities in Labrador," she said. "I think you'll find it wonderfully entertaining."

While I brushed my teeth, I looked at my eyes in the bathroom mirror. McClure eyes. Like Bea and Addie's.

Like my great-grandmother's and people in her family before her.

I put on my pajamas and got under the quilt. The sheets smelled fresh as the breeze coming in the window. I opened the book, but my McClure eyes closed before I'd read a word.

*T*he telephone woke me the next morning. I'd been dreaming about something upsetting, something I had to do.

My room was so bright with sun I couldn't see when I went into the dim hall. I felt my way down the stairs and went into the kitchen.

"*Good* morning!" Addie was wearing a red kimono over her nightgown. Bea's was purple. "That was your mother on the phone. So nice to hear Andrea's voice. She was checking to see if you arrived safely."

Mama calling, that was my dream. She'd been calling my name over and over. I'd yelled till my throat hurt, "Here, Mama, here I am!" but she didn't hear me. Her voice got farther and farther away no matter how loud I yelled.

I yawned, trying not to show how bad I felt about missing her call.

"Did she want to talk to me?" I asked.

"She said not to wake you when we told her you were still sleeping." Bea looked at me over the top of her glasses. She was working on a crossword puzzle. With a ballpoint pen, I noticed. "You can call her back. Call her anytime you want."

"I don't need to," I said, avoiding her gaze. "I'm sorry I'm late." I could see I'd missed breakfast. Mama had told me it was very important with older people to be on time for meals.

"Breakfast is self-serve whenever you want it," Addie said. "There are six kinds of cereal in the cupboard over the sink, milk in the fridge, fruit in the pantry. Or I could make eggs or French toast?" She was half on her way to do it, but I shook my head.

"Thank you. I like cereal." Six kinds were more than the Swanes had. Mama only got whole-grain cereals from the food co-op. You had to cook them forever, and even then they clumped in your stomach like a rock.

I looked at each box. "We try to keep a good selection for our guests," Addie said. "We offer them hot and cold cereals, fresh muffins, eggs, pancakes or French toast, bacon, sausage, plus of course fruit and juice. I think it's fairly adequate, but you never can be sure about the cold cereals with so many brands on the market."

"Your friends must be big eaters," I said. "We usually just have one thing at a time."

Addie laughed till her eyes watered. "We started a bed-and-breakfast a few years back," Bea explained. "People expect a hearty meal."

"We've a lovely sign out front that Ed Perry painted," Addie said. "It was probably too dark for you to notice last night. It shows the trees in the four seasons and says 'McClures' Maples.'"

"Grandfather McClure was a sea captain, you know," Bea said. "He always said that what he hankered for most after long months at sea, next to Grandmother of course, were those two maples in the front yard."

"Do lots of people come?" I poured milk on my cereal, lovely cold white milk. It looked just right swirling around the golden flakes and the banana I'd sliced on top. Mama went back and forth on whether milk was good for us or not. Lately we'd been putting fruit juice on our cereal, which didn't go with it in my opinion.

"We had four parties last season," Addie said. "Just enough to add a little interest."

"Heron Cove isn't really on the tourist trail," Bea said.

"What little shoreline we have is still mostly owned by the families of the farmers and seagoers who lived here a century ago. Vacationers sometimes find their way out here, but there's no entertainment and no place for them to spend the night, except with us. Addie and I wouldn't mind a bit more business to fatten our travel fund, but nobody here wants the tourist industry buying up the place."

"Where do you want to travel?" I asked.

"Africa," Addie answered right away.

"India first," Bea said. She squinted at the puzzle. "'Hog plum,' four letters, blank-*M*-*R*-blank."

Addie looked over Bea's shoulder. "Are you sure thirty-seven Down has an *E*?"

Africa. India. Other than my trip to Spokane, Heron Cove was the farthest I'd ever been from home.

"Have you been other places?" I asked.

"Oh yes." Addie nodded. "We've been about some. Japan, that's where we got these kimonos, and New Zealand, and most of Europe. I was in Peru last winter while Bea was on an exchange to Russia. We both went to Nicaragua in '85 to see that terrible situation for ourselves. Elliot thought we'd risked life and limb on that trip. Best we hadn't told him."

"Speaking of your grandfather," Bea said, "he called

Sunday. Your grandmother's been having more migraines. She's going in for tests."

Addie snapped the newspaper she was scanning into order. "If Helen could get her mind off herself for one minute, her migraines would surely improve."

"Now, Addie," Bea said with a glance in my direction.

She needn't have worried. I heard much worse from Mama. "Did you tell him I was coming here?" I asked.

"No, we didn't," Addie said. "As he didn't mention it, we assumed he didn't know and it wasn't for us to tell."

It seemed they were aware of the situation between Mama and her parents. I got up and lowered the drying rack for the dishcloth and towel, and did my dishes in the little sink next to the window.

"Your hair is very energetic, isn't it," Addie said. "Really quite remarkable. Certainly no Miller influence there. My own hair was dark, but Bea's showed the Miller red. All father's side was light-complected." Addie slid a sly glance at Bea.

"My hair was auburn," Bea retorted. "The Miller red was more a strawberry blond. Quite striking really," she added hastily. "Andrea's is like spun gold."

"Her hair is kind of faded now." I hesitated, then said, "Mine is like my father's."

I waited for the questions.

"Most likely so," was all Bea said.

"Quite a gift," said Addie.

I smoothed the dishcloth and towel back on the drying rack and raised it. The one time I'd said that to Mama, about my hair being like my father's, she'd laughed and said certainly not by the time she met him. But Bea and Addie, who knew the family traits, agreed with me.

I could hear a hummingbird zig and zag around the honeysuckle bush outside the window. The sea sparkled beyond the field. I felt a rush of love for this place and these aunts who liked my hair.

"I want to go across the field to the shore," I said, "and through the tunnel of trees, and then all over the house . . ."

"Good!" Addie pushed back from the table. "Let's get going."

"We were planning a tour," Bea said, "unless you want to go alone?"

I shook my head. I didn't want to let either one of them out of my sight.

$\mathcal{B}$ea went first along the path that led through the field to the sea. She stopped to point out lupine and lichen, sea rose and sedge as though they were famous places on a tour.

"She taught biology," Addie murmured from behind me. "As well as being the family historian, as you've no doubt noticed."

The breeze got stronger as we neared the water. Bursts of sweet salt tang thrilled my nose, my hair, my skin. I felt a great opening up when we came out of the tall grass and there was nothing left between us and the sea. I thought Bea and Addie felt it, too. We drifted apart, following narrow trails of sand between the rocks.

The last time I'd come through the field, I'd been holding my grandfather's hand. I'd felt that same excitement when we reached the water. He'd let me run along the narrow beach, in and out of the reaching foam, without a single "be careful." He had rolled up his pant legs and followed at a distance, his hands in his pockets, his white hair blowing back from his bald spot.

Mama wasn't with us that day. She didn't like the ocean much. Her skin burned easily, the brightness hurt her eyes, the salt made her itch. I remembered the look and feel of my grandfather's hands as he'd dried my feet with his handkerchief. He had wiped every grain of sand from between my toes before he put on my socks and tied my sneakers in double bows. That was one of the best times I'd had with my grandfather. I'd written about it in fourth grade when we were supposed to write something about one member of our family for a class history project.

Bea and Addie sat on a driftwood log while I danced along the beach. The tide was out. It looked like the seaweed-covered rocks were drying their curls in the sun. I found two starfish and a sea cucumber.

"Do you swim here?" I asked when I got back to my aunts.

"Oh no!" Addie shuddered. "It's much too cold and rocky. Some people go over to Waring Pond, but we never got in the way of it. Though of course we'd be glad to take you."

"Grandfather made us learn to swim," Bea said. She popped a pod of seaweed and examined its lining. "The summer Ernie Bond fell out of his dory and drowned, the student minister decided to give swimming lessons in the creek behind the store. What was his name, Addie?"

"Felcher. Reverend Felcher. The poor man nearly froze to death trying to get us to keep our heads above water."

"Can I swim here at high tide?" I asked.

"If you can take the cold," Bea said. "There's a strip of sandy bottom down near the end there. But be sure we're here to watch."

Going back, we took a path that led toward town.

"I don't understand why my mother doesn't come here." I was sorry the instant the words were out. The one thing I didn't want to do that day was think about my mother.

"We certainly wish she would," Bea said. "She visited now and then in the years before you were born, but never for more than a day or two. Of course, before we retired, Addie and I were here only in the summers."

"Your grandmother, Helen, never liked it here," Addie said. "She and Elliot have come a few times over the years, but generally Bea and I have visited them in Spokane. Heron Cove wasn't Elliot's home, more's the pity. As soon as he was free of the Lexfield farm, he went straight out west and stayed there. I'm sure your mother has told you all about that."

"About what?" I knew Grampa and Bea and Addie grew up on a farm not far from here in Lexfield. And Bea had told me last night that she and Addie lived with their grandparents in Heron Cove after their mother died. That was all I knew.

The look Addie and Bea gave each other said there was more to it.

"Andrea may not know all that happened," Addie murmured.

Bea nodded. "Elliot never speaks of any of it to us."

They seemed to come to a decision.

"I don't believe in secrets," Addie announced.

"Not in the family," Bea agreed. "We'll talk in the cemetery on the way back, Sage. It'll be easier to explain there."

Family secrets to be told at the cemetery. I could hardly wait. Mama and I didn't have any family stories. Not with Gramma and Grampa so far away and Mama only wanting to fuss about them anyway. Nina's family had lots of stories. Her grandfather had gambled one million dollars away on racehorses. And one of her relatives shot out his sister's eye with a bow and arrow. The sister said it had been no accident. Nina had seen the empty socket.

It didn't take long for us to cover all of Heron Cove. The only road was lined with oak trees that met overhead. A store was at one end of the trees and McClures' Maples was at the other. In between were nine old white houses, a church, and a cemetery. One of the houses, Bea said, had been the school before the consolidated one was built in Beaverton.

Kittredge, Perry, Osborne, Sims . . . Bea named each house as we passed. Addie unlocked the door of the Heron Cove United Church with a key from her household ring to show me the McClure pew and the new red carpeting, which she checked for bits of lint on the way out.

"Our grandfather started this store when he retired from the sea," Bea said when we got there. "Ina Sims runs it now."

"Brace yourself," Addie whispered to me as she pulled open the screen door with a Lipton tea sign on it. "Good morning, Ina," she said briskly to the woman behind the counter. "We'd like you to meet our Sage. She'll be with us this summer."

Our Sage. I couldn't help smiling in spite of the way

the woman was looking me over. She had stiff black curls that looked dyed, a thin red mouth, and nosy eyes.

Ina Sims's lips barely twitched a smile back. "Andrea's girl, isn't she? I don't see much likeness, though I'm not well acquainted with either Andrea or Elliot."

"She's clearly McClure," Addie said coolly.

"*I* don't see it," Ina said, and went on to tell us all about Ed Perry's bad spell in the night. We got milk and the mail, and Addie ordered a chicken for Sunday.

"Anything Ina Sims hears, the whole community will know the same day," Bea said as we started back along the sidewalk. "Just remember to watch what you say, Sage. She pries and tells, but she means no harm."

"Mean it or not, she does plenty of it," Addie said. She checked her watch. "I'll go ahead and start lunch while you two visit the cemetery." She waggled good-bye with the milk carton and left us at the graveyard gate.

*B*ack home in Hollins, the cemetery had a black marble statue everybody called Sad Agnes. It was bigger than a real woman. Sad Agnes was supposed to be sitting by the grave of her daughter, who died from influenza. She was dressed in a robe with a hood that hid her face. On Halloween, kids always dared one another to go sit on her lap. I did it once. I could see her stone eyes staring at me from inside the hood. I never went back, not even when everybody went to see Tommy Cutter's grave the summer he died.

The Heron Cove cemetery didn't have any big stat-ues. Bea talked right along in her normal voice after we'd walked through the gate in the stone wall. She led me to some graves near an old beech tree. "The McClures are all over here," she said. She pointed out three weathered gray stones. "This is Grandfather, this is Grandmother, and this is Mother."

I nodded at each, and read the inscriptions: ALEXANDER MCCLURE, SARAH BOND MCCLURE, ANNA MCCLURE MILLER. Anna was born September 8, 1889, and died April 18, 1928. She was Grampa and Bea and Addie's mother, Mama's grandmother, my great-grandmother. Her stone said OUR LAMB HAS FOUND HER WAY HOME.

"Wives and children were considered the property of the husband in those days," Bea said when I bent close to read the words. "It was something of a scandal to have Charlie, and then Mother, buried here in Heron Cove with the McClures instead of in Lexfield with the Millers."

Bea brushed fresh-cut grass from a small stone next to Anna's. "This is Charlie. Do you know anything at all about him?"

I shook my head. I knew that besides Bea and Addie, Grampa had two older brothers, Jack and Eli, who'd died a long time ago, but I'd never heard of Charlie. Bea sat down by the beech tree and patted the grass for me to join her. The midday sun polka-dotted us through the leaves. Lilac bushes and sea roses grew all over the cemetery. A chubby woman in a blue dress and a baseball cap was planting geraniums by the stone wall. An old woman wearing overalls was weeding near her.

"That's Dell MacDougal and her mother," Bea said. She waved at them, then settled back against the tree.

"Our father, Lorenzo Miller, was a harsh man," she began. "He was honest and hardworking, he was a pillar of the church, and advanced in his knowledge of farming. But there was no warmth in him, no laughter. It was probably because his mother died when he was a small boy. I don't know what kind of woman she was, but after she died, his father is said to have worked his children mercilessly. Some people from the community even tried to intervene, which was most unusual in those days. They said the children's growth was being stunted because of hard work and inadequate food. Whatever the truth of that, there's little doubt it was a miserable situation, and misery, Sage, can be tenacious. It grows fat if you give it ground."

Bea nodded toward the family of stones. "Our mother's people, the McClures, were a different story. They were warmhearted sea folk who loved music, books, and tomfoolery. I've never understood why Mother married Father. Maybe she thought she could make him happy. He wouldn't have any of it, though. He frowned on music and games, and the only book he'd allow was the Bible."

"Why?" I'd never heard of anyone against books.

"Hearts grown cold fear the sun, Sage. I've seen it in others. Maybe they just can't believe in something better, or maybe thawing is too painful. Mother did what she could. She told us stories and sang with us when Father wasn't around. She was always reciting poetry, whole long pieces when she was working in the kitchen, or lines here and there when something called them to mind. She had an amazing memory. We never doubted her tender heart or her love for us, but she was worn down by hard work and Father's rules. Her family could have been a great help and comfort to her, but Father didn't welcome their visits or make it easy for Mother to see them here in Heron Cove. Grandmother and Grandfather did come every year on her birthday with cake and homemade ice cream, and on a very rare Sunday she'd hitch up the wagon and announce that we were going to Heron Cove for the day."

"How far away was it?" I asked.

"Twelve miles," Bea said. "Not far now, but a long way then, given the circumstances. We didn't have a car in those days."

She gazed at the small stone. "Addie and I were almost five when our little brother, Charlie, was born. He was great entertainment for us, as well as for Elliot. Our older brothers, Jack and Eli, were in their teens by then, more adults than kids.

"Charlie was a happy little fellow, the delight of

Mother's heart. Maybe Father was jealous of that, for right from the start he was determined Charlie not be indulged. He had him out planting potatoes and pulling turnips along with the rest of us long before he should have been."

"Why did your mother let him go?"

I was sorry I asked, because Bea looked sad. After a while she said, "I don't know, Sage. I've wondered myself. Father was a hard man to stand up to. I think there were times Mother may have been afraid for us."

She pulled a piece of timothy grass and bit off the sweet end. "The day Charlie died, Elliot and Addie and I were at school. Father was cutting cordwood with Jack and Eli, and wanted Charlie to carry lunch to them at noon.

"It was a cold day, with snow on the ground. Mother said she'd bring the lunch, but Father said no, it wasn't far and she had other things to tend to."

Bea sighed and shook her head. "Charlie delivered the lunch all right, but he complained of stomach pains and asked if he could lie down on the sled. Father said he'd freeze lying around in those temperatures, and to get on home. Jack and Eli each asked to carry the little boy, but Father wouldn't hear of it. Charlie couldn't be a baby forever, he said."

Bea cleared her throat. "Charlie made it home, but he died that night. The doctor didn't get there until the next day. He said it could have been a burst appendix . . . we never really knew."

"Would he have died anyway?" I asked after a while. "If he hadn't taken the lunch?"

"I don't know," Bea said. "It was just all connected for us. In the end, I don't think Mother blamed Father so much for Charlie's dying as for not cherishing him while he was living. She blamed herself most of all for abiding by Father's dictates."

"Is that how Charlie got buried here?" I asked. "Because she wouldn't listen anymore?"

Bea nodded. "Father sent the boys to dig a grave in the Lexfield cemetery. You can imagine how it must have been for them. Especially Elliot. He was still a child himself. Mother went after them and told them to stop digging, that Charlie was to be buried in Heron Cove with her people. I don't know what was said between her and Father, but Grandfather McClure came that very day and brought Charlie's body here to Heron Cove. That same winter, Mother took sick. Grandfather McClure fetched her and Addie and me less than two months after Charlie died. When Mother died that spring, Grandfather saw to it that she was buried here in Heron Cove next to Charlie."

"What about Grampa?" I asked.

Bea looked at me. "That's part of the tragedy," she said quietly. "Elliot was left pretty much alone. After Mother died, our family fell apart. Addie and I continued to live with Grandmother and Grandfather. We couldn't imagine returning to Lexfield without Mother, and whether Father didn't want us or our grandparents wouldn't let us go, I can't say, but it was a true blessing for us to live here in Heron Cove with our grandparents.

"Soon after Mother's funeral, Jack and Eli went off on their own. They just disappeared. We didn't hear until years later they'd been lost at sea. Elliot was the only one left to work the farm with Father. Grandmother and Grandfather felt bad about it, but they'd done all they could. They helped him with his education after Father died, and when the Lexfield place burned, they told him he'd have a share in the house here. He wasn't much interested in that, though, and I can't say as I blame him."

Bea hesitated, then said, "You know, given the history, Addie and I often thought of changing our last name to McClure. But the truth is, whether we like it or not, we're just as much Miller as McClure, and in the end, we couldn't bring ourselves to leave Elliot the only one with the Miller name. It would have been like abandoning him all over again."

"Does my mother know all this?" I asked after a while.

"I don't know," Bea said. "Probably not, if she's said nothing to you. It's not a happy story, but it's part of us, and Addie and I feel it needs to be acknowledged. The pain echoes through the generations like an unhealed wound if you keep it hidden. Look at poor Elliot, way across the country in Spokane, trying so hard not to be the dictator our father was he's afraid to speak up at all. And Andrea, so adrift from family, avoiding connection—"

Bea stopped abruptly. "Forgive me, Sage. That's not for me to say."

But it was for her to say, because we were all family, Bea and Addie, Grampa, Mama, me, and all the other people Bea had been telling me about.

"I'll tell Mama," I said. Maybe if Mama knew what had happened when Grampa was little, she'd feel nicer about him. Maybe she'd appreciate he wasn't mean and bossy like his father had been.

"Good." Bea patted Charlie's stone once more, then held out her hand. "Help me up, Sage. It's time for lunch."

We waved good-bye to Dell MacDougal and her mother and went out the gate.

"We can't change what went before," Bea said, giving me a gentle, serious look, "but we can choose what to make of it. That's where the light lies, Sage. That's the redemption."

I thought I understood what she meant, though I couldn't have explained it in words. As we walked along home, I realized I was still holding Bea's hand. I hadn't held anyone's hand like that in a long time.

*A*fter the visit to the cemetery, I thought a lot about Charlie and Elliot and my great-grandmother Anna. Bea said that my bedroom had been Anna's when she was growing up. I imagined her sleeping there, getting dressed in the mornings, looking out the very same windows toward the sea. Bea and Addie had lived here when they were my age, and now I was here, in this same house, part of this family. It was a peaceful, contented feeling, kind of like waking up from a good dream and knowing it was real.

I wanted to talk to Mama about all this. I wanted to tell her about how sad it had been for Grampa, but mostly I wanted her to know she belonged here, too. At least once every day that week, I picked up the phone and dialed our number. Every time, I hung up before it could ring. Mama didn't seem as interested in family as I was. Plus she always tried to keep long-distance calls as short as possible. How could I tell her anything that mattered, if she wasn't wanting to listen?

What I really wanted was for Mama to call me. I wanted her to say how much she missed me, and to ask about everything I was doing. Then I could have told her I missed her, too, and about our family. But she didn't call again for over a week, when she was ready to leave for Vermont. By that time I felt all upset with her for waiting so long.

Bea and Addie were in the garden picking peas, so I was the one who answered. "Sage?" Mama said, as though we'd been together the whole time. "What a whirlwind! I've finally got the garden in, everything else is a mess, and it turns out my food is *not* included in the cost of this institute. I can't believe—"

"Hello, Mama." I interrupted her in a loud, level voice.

She hesitated. "Hello, Sage," she said. I could just see the pleasant, bland look she got when she thought she was being reasonable in a trying situation. "Did you have something you wanted to tell me?" she asked when I stayed quiet.

"No," I said. Because by then, I didn't. I wasn't going

to ask if she missed me, or why she hadn't called or written. And I didn't feel anymore like telling her the story about Grampa and Charlie and Anna, or how I felt surrounded by family here. You didn't talk about things like that with someone who was too busy to even care about her own daughter.

I could hear Mama sigh. "My poor darling," she said with great patience, "are you still sulking about all this? When I was your age, I would have given anything to be where you are right now. I do hope you're being decent to Bea and Addie."

My head went so hot my scalp itched. I scrubbed it until my hair was tumbled all over my face.

"I *love* Bea and Addie," I said. "And I love Heron Cove. I wish I could live here forever."

"There, you see?" Mama said. "Believe me, it's better than Ryegate. Listen, I just called to give you my address. I'll give you a phone number, too, but it's a central one, so use it only in an emergency." Mama read me the information, then said, "I've got to run. Love you." She gave a smacking kiss and was gone.

I wiped my cheek as though a wet kiss had actually landed there. I hung up, then picked up the receiver again and listened to the dial tone. After a while I went upstairs, got my drawing pad, and sat in the rocker. I scribbled black loops all over a page. I stared at them, then I put a stick-figure Mama holding a telephone at the top of the loops, and me at the bottom. I made Mama's mouth huge, going yakkety-yakkety-yak. I made my mouth huge, too, because I was bawling. I wanted to scrub Mama out with thick black lines, but I knew from doing that in other drawings it would make me feel worse rather that better. Instead, I drew jagged mountains and trees through the telephone coils between us.

I took my drawing pad out to where Bea and Addie were still picking peas. "Mama called," I said casually. "She leaves for her institute tomorrow. Do you want any help?"

I saw Bea's quick look of concern. "Thank you, Sage, but this is play to us." She finished her side of a row and offered me some peas. "I hope you told your mother what a help you are."

"As well as a delight," said Addie. "Are you sure you got all of them, Bea? You have to look down low."

I bit through a sweet, crisp pod. "What is Ryegate?" I asked.

My aunts looked at each other through the vines. "Ryegate?" Addie shook her head. "I'm not sure . . ."

"Mama said when she was my age, she would have given anything to be here. She said it was better than Ryegate."

Bea emptied her full basket into a bag. "Maybe it's

that school she went to," she said. "The one before Mount Holly."

"That must be it," Addie said. "Though she was older than you are, Sage, at the time. We both offered to have her stay with us, but Helen wouldn't hear of it."

"We never really knew the whole situation," Bea said, "but when your mother was about fourteen, her parents sent her to boarding school. She didn't last long at the first place. I think that may have been Ryegate."

"Little wonder," Addie said. "My understanding was it was basically a boot camp for girls. She must have told you about that, Sage."

I'd never heard one word about it. I thought my mother went to Mount Holly High School in Spokane. I'd seen her yearbook.

"Why did her parents send her there?" I asked.

Bea started on another row. "Helen said she needed more discipline than they could give her. I believe she was expelled from Ryegate—to her credit, I might venture. She was happier at Mount Holly."

"That was her high school in Spokane, right?" I'd picked out all the pictures of her in her yearbook. She'd been in the drama club, the chorus, and on the basketball team.

"It was a boarding school in northern California." Addie fanned herself with her hat. "You missed a whole bunch right there, Bea. No wonder you're so fast." She offered me a basket with far fewer peas than Bea's had.

Any other time, it would have been hard to keep a straight face. It cracked me up how competitive they were, especially Addie. I took one of her peas and said, "If you don't need me, I think I'll go down to the beach and draw."

The tide was in, like a rumpled blanket pulled up over lumpy bedsprings. I found a place to sit where I could lean against an old lobster trap. The creamy binding of the blanket reached almost to my toes.

It scared me, all this new information about Mama. I couldn't understand why she hadn't told me. She'd never actually said Mount Holly High School was in Spokane. I just naturally thought it was, since that's where she lived. I wondered what could have happened to make her parents send her away to boarding school. She must have done something pretty bad to cause that. A boy on the next street over from us in Hollins was sent away to boarding school. He took his mother's car all the time when he didn't even have a license, plus he was suspended three times for bringing alcohol to school. Nina's mother said his parents were nice people who had tried everything and were at their wit's end.

On the phone, Mama had compared my coming to Heron Cove to her being sent to Ryegate. Did that mean she'd planned her herb institute as an excuse to send me away? I knew we hadn't been getting along very well for quite a while. She'd arranged for me to see the school guidance counselor about it. Mrs. Ashford said it was a normal part of growing up, and that things were bound to be more intense when there was just the two of us. Not getting along wasn't a good-enough reason to send someone away, was it?

I closed my eyes against the brightness of the sun. A gull cried, then all was perfectly still. The light came through my eyelids, everything melted into it . . .

I opened my eyes and saw a black bird standing on a rock that stuck up from the water. Its wings were spread and its neck stretched forward. It looked the way I felt when I looked out at the ocean. I turned to a new page in my pad and drew fast. It took me a while to get the shoulders right, but the bird waited.

"It's a cormorant," Bea said when I got back and showed her the picture. "You got the posture perfectly, Sage. They often sit like that, as though they're about to take off."

Addie was mixing shortcake dough in the pantry. "Jamie Weisner's coming to mow the lawn tomorrow," she said. "Maybe the two of you could be friends. I'm afraid there aren't any other young people your age around here."

"I can mow the lawn," I said. Though it would be nice to meet this Jamie.

"I know you can, dear, but you do enough already, and Jamie likes the money." Addie rolled the dough out into a circle. "I told him to come about three so he can have tea with us."

"I may not be here," I said. I loved the tea we had together most afternoons, and I liked boys well enough. Some of them, anyway. But I'd found out that by the time you were my age, you couldn't just be friends with them anymore, and there was no point in thinking otherwise.

"What will you be doing?" Bea asked. She had a way of looking at me that made me wonder if she could tell what I was really thinking.

"I'm going to plant something around Charlie's grave," I said as though I'd planned it all along. "I noticed his didn't have any flowers."

"It's best to do it in the late afternoon," I explained when I saw Addie's eyebrows go up. "Mama says that way the plants get a chance to adjust before the sun gets too hot again."

I set out the next afternoon with a trowel and a jug of water. I went right through the cemetery gate and over to my family's stones as though I did this all the time. My family. The thought filled me to the brim.

I left my things by Charlie's grave and went on to the store. Mrs. Perry had been selling her leftover plants there for twenty-five cents each. They were lined up outside by the steps. As I tried to decide what would look good together, Ina Sims came to the door.

"I should think Bea and Addie had enough flowers already." The way she said it made them sound greedy.

I picked out a pot of bright blue lobelia before looking up at her. "They're for the cemetery." I was surprised when she came out and picked up a feathery plant with golden yellow flowers. "That lobelia is my favorite," she said. "This single-petal marigold would go well with it."

I nodded. "Now something red," I said. Ina found a geranium she thought would be red when it bloomed. I chose another lobelia to make an even dollar and carried the plants back to the cemetery in a carton she gave me.

I was thinking about my grandfather, Elliot, as I dug the grass from the front edge of Charlie's stone. He must have felt very bad when his mother took his sisters to Heron Cove and left him behind in Lexfield with a mean father. The reasons for it, that his mother was sick and he was older than Bea and Addie, still wouldn't have made it any easier for him.

I arranged the plants in the cleared patch, and watered them. Then I weeded around the other family stones and dug up a small rose shoot for the new patch. By the time I finished, I had an idea about something I might do for my grandfather.

I was so excited about my plan, I forgot all about Jamie Weisner. Just as I came out of the tunnel of trees to our lawn, the mower roared around the far side of the house. Addie must have been watching, because she came right out to meet me.

"There you are, dear. I'm glad you're back. Jamie's

just finishing up. Jamie!" she shouted, holding on to me with one hand and trying to get the boy's attention with the other. "Jamie, for heaven's sake, shut that thing off and MEET SAGE." The last words shouted into sudden silence as Jamie saw us and leaped to kill the motor.

He pulled off his earphones. "I'm sorry, Ms. Addie, there's this great discussion on public radio about this guy who injects nitrogen—"

"Jamie," Addie interrupted, "I want you to meet our niece, Sage Miller. Sage, this is Jamie Weisner. He lives—"

"—out off the shore road." Jamie grabbed my hand with his sweaty one and pumped it. "How do you do," he said, pumping away. "I've seen you around. I would have said hello, but I was always pushing somebody's mower. So how do you like it here so far?"

"I like it." I tried to dry my hand on my shorts without him noticing.

"Good." Jamie nodded seriously, his straight hair flopping in his eyes. "It can be lonely in Heron Cove for a young person."

"Are *you* lonely?" I asked. He didn't look much older than I was.

Jamie grinned. "Never," he said. "Not here."

Already it was obvious that Jamie wasn't like any boy I'd ever met.

"Come along," Addie urged. "The tea will get cold."

I thought I was a little taller than Jamie as we washed our hands at the kitchen sink. His freckles were so thick the sunburned skin between them looked like fresh scars. "So," I said, "this guy who injects nitrogen. Is he the same one with the special microscope who says he can cure cancer?"

Jamie stared at me. "Where did you hear about him? He says he's had all these good results, but he can't get any recognition from the medical establishment. Hello, Ms. Bea." Jamie beamed a big-toothed grin at her, then turned back to me.

"My mother's into that alternative-medicine stuff." I slid into my chair at the table. "Yum!" I said as Addie put a plate of strawberry shortcake in front of me. "Where did you get the berries?"

"Beaverton," Bea said. "First of the season. They're always a little ahead of us. Tell us what you've been doing, Jamie. We haven't seen you in a while."

Jamie told us about a kayak his mother had found at a yard sale. "I can carry it myself," he said. "It's perfect for the creek and along the shore." He glanced at me. "We could take turns with it, Sage."

Before I could say anything about that, he went on to talk about an article his father was writing about St. James Bay. That reminded me of something I'd read in the Grenfell book Bea gave me. Then Bea told us about how you can find out the cause of death from a skeleton, and Addie got into an analysis of the influence of geography on the Red Sox and their fans. The conversation, I thought, was kind of like music. Lots of parts that all went together.

"What are you thinking about, Sage?" Jamie's question was so unexpected, I answered before I had time to think how strange it might sound.

"That my stomach doesn't hurt."

It was suddenly quiet. Then: "Has your stomach been bothering you?" Bea asked. "You didn't tell us you felt sick!" Addie said.

"No! I don't!" I said. "It's just sometimes when I'm eating and there's lots of talk . . ." I often got stomach-aches at home, but I'd just been noticing that I hadn't had a single one since coming to Heron Cove. Maybe it was because Mama listened to the news when we were getting supper, then she ranted on about it while we were eating.

"I know what you mean," Jamie said. "It depends on who you're with and what you're talking about. It must have something to do with the release of digestive fluids. It would be interesting to look that up, the relationship between emotional states and the process of digestion, because obviously they *are* related, I just don't know how."

As he mulled it over, Jamie took a bite of shortcake

that left a streak of whipped cream between his right nostril and his mouth. I tried not to laugh, but I couldn't help it.

"What?" Jamie grinned, which made me laugh harder. Addie reached across to wipe the streak away with her napkin. "For heaven's sake, Sage," she scolded, "mind your manners. The poor boy isn't going to take tea with us if you behave like that."

"I'm sorry," I gasped. "It's just . . . that it looked like—"

"We know what it looked like," Addie interrupted hastily. She frowned at Bea, who was laughing as hard as I was. "You're no better than she is."

"Your aunts are the greatest," Jamie said later, when we were sitting out on the steps. "My mom says they are real role models."

"How long have you known them?" I asked.

"We moved here summer before last," Jamie said. "My mother teaches chemistry at the University of Maine in Orono. She and Bea like to talk science. We live in Orono in the school year, and Bea and Addie stay with us when they come for lectures or concerts. My dad writes for magazines. When he's not traveling, he works here."

I took hold of the end of one braid and studied it. "My dad's a geologist." I slowly unwound the elastic from the braid and watched the hair spring free. My hands were shaking and my breath felt shaky, too.

"He died last winter," I said.

Jamie looked at me. "I'm sorry," he said quietly.

I nodded, and released the other braid. "Listen," I said. "I have to go."

"Okay." Jamie was still watching me. "I mow the church lawn tomorrow. I'll stop after and see if you want to do something."

He went into the house to say good-bye to my aunts while I ran for the path to the sea.

It was the first time I had said that to anyone. *My father died.*

$\mathcal{M}$y father died on December 3. He was already dead when I was choosing Christmas presents that I imagined sending him from the L.L. Bean catalog.

I found out about it at supper on January 21, forty-nine days later. All that time, I didn't know.

"I was reading a newsletter on the Internet today," Mama said, "and I saw that Robert Kastenberg died."

I kept right on eating, because of course she couldn't be talking about *my* Robert Kastenberg. Not my *father*. Not all mixed up like that with the other news of her day.

"He was a good man," she said. "Only sixty-four. What a shame."

I think that's when I started hating her. I was hating her right now as I sat hunched up on the cormorant rock.

Bea and Addie stayed at Jamie's house whenever they went to Orono. They'd never stayed at my house, because Mama never invited them. She hadn't told me much about them either. Just like she hadn't told me much about my father.

My father didn't know anything at all about me. He never even knew I was alive. He didn't know I was his daughter, because Mama never told him.

Mrs. Ashford at counseling was the only one who wanted to talk about my father's dying. I told her it didn't bother me. When she kept bringing it up, I stopped going to see her. I didn't know what to say about someone I'd never met. I wasn't going to tell her how I pretended about him and his family. I just didn't want to talk to her about any of it.

I wondered if Mama had mentioned in her letter to Bea and Addie that my father died. Probably not. He wasn't important to her, and she didn't think he was important to me. She told Mrs. Ashford I could hardly grieve someone I never met. She didn't know I thought about him and his family all the time. She didn't know I cut out a "Dear Abby" column from the newspaper that said how to find missing people. I had it with me here in Heron Cove, folded behind the ID card in my wallet.

Maybe Mama didn't tell Bea and Addie, but Jamie did. They were out by the path watching for me when I came back across the field.

Bea took my hand. "Jamie told us you were upset about your father. We're so sorry, Sage."

Addie took the other hand. "We didn't know he died, dear. You must have thought us awful louts not to speak of it."

I wanted to say *That's okay, nobody spoke of it,* but I choked on a rush of tears. They held me close as wails and sobs tore out of me.

"I loved him," I finally managed to say. "He was my father. I never met him, but I loved him."

"Of course you did," Addie said. "You always will."

Bea wiped my face with her handkerchief and held it for me to blow my nose. "Such a loss," she murmured. "Such a terrible loss."

They took care of me as though I were sick. I guess I was. My nose got all sore from crying, and my head ached. I felt too tired even to read, and I was cold. I lay in the sun, wrapped in my quilt, and slept.

Addie brought meals to me in bed. She fixed little things, like cocoa and toast, and custard, and baked potato with butter. Bea brushed my hair very gently and rubbed Vitamin-E oil under my nose. Whenever I woke up, one of them was near.

Addie said Jamie came twice on the second day. He brought some daisies he picked and his old Winnie-the-Pooh books. He said he still liked to read them when he felt bad.

I got up for supper that night. It was raining, so after the dishes were done Addie read to us about Eeyore losing his tail. I sat up close to her on the sofa while Bea worked on her quilt squares.

"Wonderful!" Bea said when Addie finished. "Read another."

So Addie read about Eeyore's birthday, and then about Pooh getting stuck in Rabbit's door.

"I like Jamie," I said when Addie put the book down.

"We do, too," Bea said. "He's a good friend."

"I had a friend named Robbie Fiske," I said. "We used to build forts and ride bikes and stuff. Now he won't even look at me."

"What happened?" Addie asked.

"His brother went by when we were sorting baseball cards on my front porch last summer. He made dumb noises, and asked if Robbie had kissed me yet. After that, Robbie didn't want to do stuff anymore. Mama said it's hard for boys and girls to be friends when you get older."

"I don't think you'll find that's true with Jamie," Bea said.

"I certainly hope not," Addie said. "Ezra Kittredge was one of my best friends from the time I was ten until he died four years ago. So it's quite possible, you see."

"Wait a minute," I said. I ran upstairs and opened the little drawer of the bed table. I kept the picture wrapped in Kleenex for protection.

I ran back downstairs and handed it to Bea.

"This is my father," I said.

Bea went and sat next to Addie on the sofa so she could see it, too. They looked at it carefully.

"Fetch the magnifying glass on the desk, please, Sage," Bea said, and they looked at it through that.

"He has a nice presence about him," Bea said.

"He does." Addie nodded. "From what I can see, I would say you have his mouth, Sage."

Bea looked at mine closely. "Definitely his mouth, yes. A lovely, generous-looking mouth." She handed the picture back. "Thank you for showing us that, Sage. I wonder if you'd like to protect it in a frame?"

I nodded. I was crying again, but this time it felt better.

We took my father's picture to Beaverton the next morning, where I found a silver frame that looked really good with it. When we got home, we had a memorial service for him, just the three of us. I carried his picture down to the shore and put it on the cormorant rock. We looked at the picture and out at the water while Addie read a poem that said how everything, like alive and dead people, the stars, and the sea, was part of everything else. Then Bea said, "We give thanks for the life of Robert Kastenberg. And we thank you, Robert, for this precious child, Sage." She and Addie both said, "Amen." I put some lupine I'd picked on the way through the field next to his picture. All I said was, "Daddy." I didn't need to say anything else, because I talked to him in my heart.

After lunch, I started on the plan I'd thought of for my grandfather when I was putting flowers by Charlie's grave. I made a list of things I wanted to draw: the store, the sidewalk going through the tunnel of oak trees, the sea-rose hedge around the garden, my room, the little brass clock on top of the bookshelves in the hall. I took my drawing pad with me that evening when I went to water the new plants in the cemetery.

I had the first drawings ready by the end of the week. I wrote a letter to send with them. I'd never written Grampa except for thank-you notes after birthdays and Christmas. I wrote on scrap paper first, then I copied it on nice paper and drew a border around it with colored pens.

Dear Grampa,
Here are some pictures I drew of things in Heron
Cove. I drew the cormorant and the lobster trap
and the flying gull at the shore where you took me
when I was six. I also drew a picture of the flowers
I planted by Charlie's grave in the cemetery. I will
draw more pictures and send them. I am staying
with Bea and Addie while my mother studies herbs.
Please give my love to Gramma.

Love from Sage
xoxo

I asked Bea and Addie for a big envelope. "I'm sending some pictures to Grampa," I said. "I wrote him a letter, too, and told him I was staying here while Mama studies herbs."

"Good," Addie said as she rummaged through the desk drawer. "I didn't like him not knowing you were here. This should do it. Just stick on a new address label."

Bea looked at my drawings through her half-glasses. "These will mean a lot to him, Sage. A very great deal indeed."

"Looks important," Ina Sims said, when she weighed the envelope for postage. She eyed me and waited.

"It is," I said. When she saw I wasn't going to tell her any more, she gave me her flared-nostrils, tight-mouth look. "That will be eighty-three cents." She stamped the envelope hard and handed me our mail. "Nothing yet from your mother."

It was plain mean of her to say that. I *was* always hoping for a letter from Mama, but it was none of Ina Sims's business. I didn't think it was even legal for her to pay attention to what mail people got.

I waited until I got to the cemetery wall to open a letter from Nina. I'd already gotten three from her, and one from Aunt Nan. Nina said day camp wasn't much fun without me. She said Robbie Fiske came up to her at the pool and asked where I was. She sent me a bookmark she'd made by ironing a pansy between pieces of waxed paper.

We had our first bed-and-breakfast guests that night. Mr. and Mrs. Belden from Utica, New York, came when it was almost dark. They wanted to see the room before they decided to stay.

"We got off track trying to find something near the water," Mr. Belden said as he bounced lightly on the edge of the guest-room mattress. He took off his shoes and lay flat. "I had no idea there were undeveloped areas like this on the coast."

"There's a shower with running hot and cold," his wife called from the bathroom. "I think we should take it, Donald."

"Not that they have a choice at this hour," Addie murmured in my ear, then said briskly, "Sage can help you with your things. Come join us in the kitchen when you're settled."

Mr. Belden and I carried up six bags. Mrs. Belden arranged them by size under the window and opened them all up. I sat at the top of the stairs until they were ready to come with me to the kitchen.

"Mother and I don't usually snack in the evenings," Mr. Belden said. He sounded like he didn't think it was a good idea, but they sat right down and finished off half a loaf of Addie's oatmeal bread and a plateful of Bea's chocolate coconut squares.

In the morning the Beldens had hot cereal, eggs, sausage, and pancakes. "Just a few, now," Mr. Belden said when Addie asked if she should mix up more pancake batter. When they were finished, Mr. Belden got out a pocket atlas and traced the routes of all the trips they'd taken since their kids grew up. Mrs. Belden told us what they'd eaten along the way. She gave me a squashed York peppermint patty from her purse when they left.

"Good eaters," Addie said as we waved good-bye.

"Oh, my!" was all Bea said.

I helped change the sheets and hang out the laundry. Then I packed a lunch and got Addie's three-speed bike I'd been using from the garage. I stopped at the end of the driveway where Bea was weeding her nasturtiums.

"Jamie and I are going to ride out the shore road to look for raspberries," I said. "I'll be back before tea."

"Wait a minute." Bea went in the house and came back with a sack of peas and lettuce and a wet paper towel. She picked a handful of nasturtiums and wrapped their stems in the paper towel. "Take these to Elizabeth," she said. "And tell Ben the rototiller's fixed whenever he wants to use it."

Jamie's parents had stopped to meet me when they'd

been out for one of their walks. I'd liked them the minute I saw them. Mr. Weisner had curly gray hair and a beard. His bright blue eyes and rimless half-glasses reminded me of Santa Claus. The first time I met him, he'd been wearing one of the shirts I'd picked out of the L.L. Bean catalog for my father. Mrs. Weisner had brown eyes and freckles like Jamie. She talked fast like him, too, as though she couldn't wait to tell you something.

Mrs. Weisner was at the mailbox by the road when I got there. She peered into the bag I gave her. "Peas and lettuce! And nasturtiums!" She carried all of it through to the screened porch, where Mr. Weisner was typing away on his computer. "Ben, look what Sage brought us!"

Mr. Weisner took the flowers his wife held out to him. "Nasturtiums," he said, touching the petals gently. "My grandmother always grew these." He separated out three. He tucked one into Mrs. Weisner's hair, one into mine, and one behind his own ear. "Jamie was looking for you a minute ago," he said. "I think he's down by the creek."

"I'm late," I said, feeling a bit breathless from the way he'd carefully put the flower in my hair. "We had bed-and-breakfast guests last night."

"Jamie!" Mrs. Weisner bellowed from the end of the porch. "Sage is here."

"Where were your guests from?" Mr. Weisner asked.

"Utica, New York," I said. "But they travel a lot. They eat a lot, too."

Mrs. Weisner laughed, "So Addie said on the phone this morning. She said they filled you in on every single trip they'd taken in their forty-three years of marriage, and ate like they were coming off a starvation diet. Here he is." She waved as Jamie came bounding across the lawn. "I hope you two have a super-elagorgeous outing."

It was a cloudless day with hardly a breeze. We ate our lunch on the rocks where the road curved close to the water at Frenchman's Cove, then followed it past the turn to Lexfield. I hadn't been beyond Frenchman's Cove before; seeing the sign for Lexfield all unexpected was like a fist to my stomach. This must have been the road Anna had taken on those Sundays she was desperate to see her parents. It was the way her father would have gone when he went to get Charlie's body and when he took her back to Heron Cove when she was sick. It wouldn't have been paved back then.

Jamie and I had to go farther than we expected to find any berries ripe enough to pick. By the time we got back to town, we were tired and hot. We went straight to Sims's store and propped our bikes by the steps.

"Afternoon, Ms. Sims," Jamie called as we headed for the freezer at the back of the store. We were trying to decide between grape, lime, or orange Popsicles when Irene Perry came in to get the afternoon paper.

"It's a hot one," we heard her say. "Saw those kids tear by a minute ago. I don't know how they keep up the pace in this heat. I'm hard-pressed to drag myself over here, but Ed's leg is troubling bad, and it helps if he has the sports and obits to look at."

"Those kids would do well to slow down all around." Ina Sims's lowered voice nailed our attention. "Their folks seem to see no need for supervision. It doesn't surprise me, the Weisners, but Bea and Addie . . ."

I could feel my face go hot and my scalp tingle. Jamie put a hand on my arm.

"Oh, for heaven's sake, Ina," Mrs. Perry said. "They're just kids having fun. I could use a little myself these days."

"Precisely my point." Ina's voice dripped with suggestion. I itched to squeeze her neck till her beady eyes popped. She was as bad as Robbie Fiske's brother.

Jamie still held my arm. "She means sex," he whispered as the screen door banged behind Irene Perry.

I looked at his matter-of-fact brown eyes and couldn't help laughing. Ina Sims's words were suddenly just dumb and silly.

"We heard what you said," I told her when we paid for our Popsicles.

"Well, don't little pitchers have big ears." Ina didn't

look at me. "Eavesdropping can get you into trouble, missy."

I kept right on looking at her. "It's mean to say stuff you don't know anything about."

"Good for you!" Addie said when Jamie and I told about it at tea. "It's about time Ina was held accountable for that tongue of hers. You two pay her no heed. A person's view is focused by what they want to see, and Ina Sims has always wanted to see a man at her door."

"Now, Addie, you don't know that. You sound as bad as she does," Bea said.

"I do, too, know that," Addie said firmly. "It's perfectly obvious from the way she simpers when a man walks into the store. She has some nerve to start in on Sage and Jamie, the old . . ." Addie pressed her lips together in a show of self-restraint.

"How come you never married?" Jamie asked, looking from Bea to Addie with great interest.

"I never found a man to suit me," Addie said. "It's as simple as that."

"My young man was killed in the war," Bea said. "I just never felt that way about anybody again."

"Statistics indicate," Jamie said, "that marriage generally benefits men more than women. My mother says you two are examples of how well women can do on their own."

I thought about how much better Anna's life would have been if she hadn't been ruled by her husband. My mother didn't have a husband, but I wouldn't have said she was exactly doing well on her own, not the way she was always wanting something else. I couldn't imagine Gramma surviving without Grampa, but it seemed to me he might have been better off if he didn't have to wait on her hand and foot and could get a word of his own in now and then.

Then there were the Weisners. They each had their own work, and in the school year they even lived separate places during the week. But Jamie told me that weekends and summers they never made plans that didn't include them both. They laughed and talked together like best friends, and I'd seen them look at each other like it was their favorite view.

"It probably depends on a lot of things," I said, after everybody had already gone on to another subject.

*E*very few days, Bea and Addie sent me off to the neighbors with sacks of vegetables from the garden. I loved having a reason to knock on the doors of the big old houses between us and the store. Even before meeting me, everybody knew who I was. They all had flower gardens, but nobody else seemed to grow vegetables.

"We let Bea and Addie supply us," Mrs. Kittredge told me the first time I brought her some peas. "Ever since they retired back here, they've gone whole hog with that garden of theirs. They plant far more than they can eat, and rely on us to help them with the surplus. We're all mighty grateful, I'll tell you that. I try to do for them when I can, but those two are always two steps ahead of me."

Mr. Perry was usually sitting on his front porch with his leg propped up. He had diabetes and his circulation was bad. "Vegetables," he said one morning when I came up the steps. "I don't believe in them. But that wife of mine makes me eat them anyway, like I was a little kid."

"You quit your fussing and thank the good Lord you've got a wife will put up with you, Ed Perry," Irene Perry said, opening the screen door. "Come on in and have a molasses cookie, Sage. Lena Osborne and I are having a cup of tea while we do the flowers for Sunday service. You can leave her vegetables here."

"What have we got today?" Mrs. Osborne took the sack I handed her and peered inside. "Oh, good, Bea put in some of her basil. And arugula. I know you don't care for that, Irene, but I think it makes a salad."

Mrs. Perry passed me the plate of cookies. "Your aunts know our tastes, Sage. I never get arugula, but they give me plenty of spinach, which Lena here doesn't care for."

"Leave them to their chitchat and come play a game of checkers with me, young lady," Mr. Perry called from the porch. "And bring one of those cookies with you."

Irene Perry rolled her eyes and fetched two cookies from a package marked SUGAR-FREE. She fixed a little tray with a cup of tea and handed it to me. "If you would be so good, Sage," she said. "I'll rescue you as soon as we've finished with the flowers."

I liked playing checkers with Mr. Perry. He was younger than Bea and Addie, but he remembered their grandparents, Alexander and Sarah McClure.

"Tell me about my great-great-grandparents," I said after I made my first move.

"Trying to break my concentration, are you?" He slid a checker forward with a long, big-knuckled finger. "Well, let's see now. Miz McClure, of course she was old by the time I knew her, but beautiful, still beautiful. You look something like her, if I remember right. Always kind to us kids, and she did love a good laugh. We had a minister over to the church was as dull as could be, read every word of his sermons without a glance up to see if he was still talking to anybody or if we'd all had the good sense to get up and go home. Well, one Sunday, your great-great grandma Sarah had had about enough. Before the service, she passed by the pulpit and calm as a cucumber took the bottom pages from the pile the preacher'd put there all ready to read. When he come to the end of the pages, well, he started looking this way and that, patting his robe, pulling it open to go through his pockets. 'Ahem,' he says, 'a-hem,' the whole time he's searching. When he comes up with nothing, he gathers his wits and says, 'And thus is the word of the Lord, Amen.' Your grandmother wouldn't take credit, but some saw her up there before service and didn't think it entirely out of character."

I could imagine Addie doing something like that, though she'd pretend to be as mystified as anybody about the whole thing. I jumped three of his men with my king, and said, just to keep him going, "Did my grampa Alexander think it was funny?"

"Well, now, I can't speak with certainty what your grandfather's thinking was at that particular moment, but I can tell you if Sarah did it, he'd think it a fine idea. He let me sweep out the store for him, run small errands when I was just a tyke, pay me like I was worth something. Young as I was, I'd notice how he'd light up when she came in. He was one fine sea captain, from all I hear, but on land he took Sarah's word for what ought to be."

I was two moves from cornering his final king when the women came out with three large vases of flowers.

"Ha!" Mr. Perry said, rubbing his hands together in glee. "Guess we won't have time to see how this plays out."

"Would you help Lena get these over to the church?" Mrs. Perry asked me. "Ed's got a doctor's appointment in Beaverton."

I stood up and took a vase. "Thanks for the game," I said to Mr. Perry. He winked at me, and I grinned. We both knew it was the stories that mattered.

The church was cool and smelled of bayberry candles. Mama wasn't much for going to church, but I liked sitting in the McClure pew on Sunday mornings with Bea and Addie. The minister was a woman who came over from Beaverton. Our service was at nine, so she could get back to her other church in time for their eleven-o'clock service.

Mrs. Osborne set the vases on stands at the front of the church. As we were on our way out, she said, "I don't know that I've ever told anybody this, but I was kind of sweet on your grandfather, Elliot, at one time, Sage. You don't look like him, but you have a way that reminds me a bit."

"You knew my grandfather?" I looked at her in surprise. "Did you live in Lexfield, too?"

Mrs. Osborne laughed. "Oh no, I've lived right here in Heron Cove for the better part of my life. I was Lena MacDougal then. There were a few years there after his father died, though, I saw quite a bit of Elliot. He'd come to town occasionally for Sunday dinner with his grandparents and call on me. Then, of course, all the young people for miles around went to the Saturday-night dances at the Lexfield Town Hall. Elliot was taking courses at the university as well as keeping some of the farm going, but he never missed one of those dances. I was quite the sad Suzie, I can tell you, when he went out west after his place burned."

I could hardly wait for lunch, when I would have both Bea and Addie's undivided attention.

"Did you know," I asked, when Addie had finished ladling vegetable soup into our bowls, "that Grampa used to go out with Mrs. Osborne?"

"I did not know that." Bea stopped buttering her roll. "I knew they were acquainted, most people from around here are. But no, I never heard they were seeing each other."

"He'd call on her when he came to dinner with your grandparents. And she saw him at the dances at the Lexfield Town Hall."

"Addie and I were going to school in Boston by then, working summers on Martha's Vineyard," Bea said. "If our grandparents knew of any courtship, they never let on in their letters." She looked at Addie. "Did Lena ever say a word to you about seeing Elliot?"

Addie shook her head. "I'm glad to hear it, though. Shows Elliot had *some* sense when it came to women. He would have done better to stick with her. She would have been better off, too, when it comes to that. Lon Osborne was no prize."

As we ate, I told them the story about their grandmother taking the sermon pages.

It was the first time I was the one who had family stories to tell.

Looks like you've got something from your grandfather," Ina Sims said about a week after I'd mailed my drawings to him.

His handwriting on the blue envelope was as pretty as Bea's. I tucked it inside the other mail and ran all the way to the cemetery wall.

My Dear Sage,
I thank you for the pictures you sent to me. I re-
member that lobster trap, or one very like it. I have
seen the gull swoop and the cormorant look to sea,
just as you have drawn. You draw very well. I used

to draw, too, years ago when I was a boy. I had
forgotten. I hid my drawings in the ticking of
my mattress. I'm sure those straw mattresses went
like tinder when the house burned.

I'm very happy to know that you are in Heron
Cove with Bea and Addie. I think of you often.

Your grandmother sends her love, along with
mine.

Grampa

xo

P. S. Charlie would have liked the yellow marigolds
you planted by his grave. Yellow flowers, especially
dandelions, were his favorite.

I put the letter back in the envelope and ran the rest
of the way home.

"I got a letter from Grampa!" I shouted as I came
through the screen door. Bea was watering the African
violets in the bay window. "He says he used to draw, too.
He hid his pictures in his mattress." I was all out of
breath. I read the letter through again before I handed it
to her.

"Addie," Bea called when she'd read it. "Addie, come
read this."

They stared at each other when Addie had finished.

"It's tickling something," Bea said.

"Yes," Addie thought for a minute, her hand over her eyes. "That envelope. In Mother's box."

"The one with school papers?" Bea said. "We told Elliot about those, but he didn't seem to want them."

"There may have been some drawings in his packet. I don't know that he ever went through things there. We certainly haven't looked at them in years."

"Let's take a peek now." Bea was already starting up the stairs.

"What are we looking for?" I asked as I followed them up to the attic.

"Mother's box," Bea said. "It's in Grandfather's old sea trunk.

"We really should bring this downstairs," Addie said as she raised the heavy curved lid of a brass-trimmed trunk. "It's too nice to leave up here."

"You will have it one day, Sage," Bea said. She lifted out two leather-bound ship's logs. There was also a dark blue wool jacket, a box with silverware tucked into velvet slots, and a black satin dress with flounces and beads. "Grandmother's Boston dress," Addie said, taking it out of its flannel wrapping and holding it up against herself.

At the bottom of the trunk was a mahogany box. It was carved all over in miniature scenes of mountains and birds and houses with lacy roofs. "Grandfather brought this from the Orient when Mother was a little girl," Bea said. "She kept her treasures in it right to the end."

"Let's take it downstairs," Addie said. "The light's too dim up here." We carefully laid the other things back in the trunk and went down to the dining room. Bea set the box on the table and opened it with a stubby brass key that was taped to the bottom. Inside were yellowed letters with ink gone brown; locks of hair wrapped in tissue and labeled with the names and ages of Anna's children; news clippings from the *Beaverton Post;* a flower, still purple, pressed into a flat star; and a child's gold ring.

A thick packet tied with green embroidery thread fit the bottom of the box. Bea sorted through folded papers tied with more of the same green thread. "Here it is." She separated out a section marked ELLIOT.

The drawings were there, underneath some school papers.

"Look." Addie gently smoothed open a small piece of brittle wrapping paper. "There's Belle eating the willow leaves. That's the horse we rode, Sage. She could be trusted with children. And here's Wrangler . . ." Addie paused, cleared her throat, and handed the drawing to Bea.

"Yes indeed." Bea studied the drawing of a large, shaggy dog sitting alert under a row of trees. "Rangler used to fetch us from school every afternoon. He'd wait like that under the trees at the edge of the school yard."

"This must have been in the maple outside the boys' window." Addie showed me a drawing of a bird's nest with three eggs. One of the eggs was starting to crack. What looked to me like a robin was perched on the edge of the nest. The other parent watched from a branch above.

There were dramatic pictures of ships in stormy seas, and one of a Model-T Ford. The last drawing was on the back of a math lesson. "It's the school Christmas tree," Bea said. "Remember, Addie? Miss McKinnon had some of the older boys cut it and bring it in. We made paper chains and strung popcorn and dipped butternuts in gold and silver paint. I'd never seen anything like it."

Addie pointed. "Look. There's my red hair ribbon. I tied it on a branch right in front and thought it was the crowning glory. We had a school party and the whole community came. Mother brought the sugar cookies she made only at Christmas. Remember Riley Waters and those cookies, Bea?"

Bea laughed. "Riley had a bit of a drinking problem," she explained to me. "He was generally a very shy man, but he'd fortify himself with a few nips to show up any-where there was free food. At our school party, he'd drunk a bit too much and said something quite bold to Edna Butterfield. I think he was more stunned than she was. He apologized profusely and blamed it all on the vanilla extract in Mother's cookies. How Mother laughed. . . ."

Bea took her glasses off and sighed. "It's odd to think that was just before Charlie died."

"It's the last of Elliot's pictures." Addie carefully returned them to order. "I never saw him draw, did you, Bea?"

Bea shook her head. "No, but Mother must have. And she must have known about his hiding place, too. She thought to save these even though she was sick and grieving when she left Lexfield. Elliot apparently never missed them; she probably knew he wouldn't have the chance to."

Mama saved my drawings in the third drawer of her desk.

"Are we going to send them to him?" I asked.

"Yes," Bea said. "Of course. Better late than never, I guess."

Addie stood up and flexed her shoulders. "We'll repack Mother's box, then we'll find something sturdy to mail these in. I don't think they'd survive much handling."

After lunch, when the pictures had been wrapped and mailed, I went to my room. I sat in the rocker and turned to a clean sheet in my pad. Instead of drawing, I wrote a letter to Mama. I told her about the Weisners and the neighbors and some of the things I'd been doing. At the end, I told her we'd found some pictures Grampa drew when he was a little boy. I said his mother had saved them, just like she saved mine.

It was the first letter I'd written to Mama since I came to Heron Cove.

*I*t was an unusually hot and dry summer. Good for business, Addie said after our third set of bed-and-breakfast guests left. They were father and son, bicycling up the coast together. Both of them looked pretty old to me. They said they'd be back in the fall to eat more of Addie's homemade bread and listen to the stories she read in the evening.

Even with the heat, the ocean was too cold to swim in. Jamie and I spent most afternoons playing with his kayak in the creek behind his house. One of us would sit in it and the other would float on an inner tube tied to the stern. We could drift most of the way to where the creek flowed into the cove, then we had to paddle and kick against the current the whole way back.

Addie and Bea sometimes came to sit with their feet in the water and visit Jamie's parents. I liked hearing their voices long after we'd drifted out of sight. We never knew what we'd find around the next bend of the creek. Once we saw a heron fishing, and another time two otters were playing in a whirlpool. At one place, the branches of an overhanging tree made a lacy green curtain around a pool that was deep enough to swim in.

"I wish you lived here always," Jamie said one afternoon as we paddled back up the creek. We were towing a lobster buoy I'd found at the cove. I thought Nina might like it. She'd never been to Maine and wanted me to bring her stuff.

"Me, too. But I still have lots of time." As soon as I said it, I knew it wasn't true. Mama's institute ended in two weeks. Even if she didn't come for me right away, school started at the end of the month.

"You could, couldn't you?" Jamie turned in the kayak to look at me. "Stay here with Bea and Addie?"

"Keep paddling!" I puffed. "We're going backward!" I *could* probably stay with Bea and Addie. It wasn't the first time I'd thought about it. But the summer had seemed forever, and suddenly it didn't.

I felt shivery in spite of the sun on my back as I pedaled my bike home. How could I leave this place? Every morning I rushed downstairs just to be with Bea and Addie. I loved every step of the way through the field to the sea. I loved tending my family's graves in the cemetery; I loved bringing vegetables to the neighbors; I loved going to the store and seeing what Ina Sims had to say. Already I knew some of the people here better than I knew people on my street in Hollins. Nobody in Hollins knew how I felt about my father, but here Bea and Addie and Jamie did. Jamie was very interested that my dad had been a geologist, because that was one of the things he was thinking about being. He had a rock collection all labeled and laid out on shelves at the end of his porch.

"Don't get ahead of yourself," Mama was always telling me. I had at least two more weeks in Heron Cove. But by the time I turned into our driveway, just thinking about leaving had me feeling as shaken as the buoy that was leaping and banging in the bike basket.

I could tell Bea was watching me out of the corner of her eye as I helped her slice a platterful of garden vegetables for supper. Addie had made macaroni and cheese, but I could eat only a few bites.

"I should think you'd be hungry after a day on the creek," Bea said.

"I had a big lunch," I said.

"It's Elizabeth and Ben's anniversary, isn't it?" Addie asked. "Did you get in on the celebration?"

I nodded. "Jamie's dad made a three-layer chocolate cake, and we had lobster rolls. His mom packed a cooler for us so they could have their lunch in privacy."

Bea laid the back of her hand against my forehead, checking for fever. She picked up my plate and scraped the untouched macaroni back into the casserole. "I'm going to let you two clean up while I water the new lettuce," she said. "All this heat's discouraging my fall crop."

I tried to read when we finished in the kitchen, but I couldn't concentrate. I went out and wandered around the house and the yard. I wondered how the light would look through the bay window after the maples lost their leaves. I imagined snow flattening the field, snow dissolving into the sea, snow shoveled in a neat path from the kitchen to the garage. I would keep the driveway shoveled. It was too much for my aunts to do.

"Where do you put your Christmas tree?" I asked them as they sat in the parlor with the day's crossword puzzle. "Do any kids come at Halloween?" I asked the next time I passed through.

The evening itself was restless. A strange quiet was disturbed by sudden stirrings of the maples and silent rips of heat lightning.

"Let's walk down through the field." Bea put the puzzle aside as I circled through the parlor a third time. "We seem to be at sixes and sevens here."

"The light's too gone for you to risk uneven ground with your bad knee, Bea," Addie said firmly.

"All right, we'll walk along the sidewalk, though it's your hip needs tending, not my knee."

I was careful not to look at either of them so they wouldn't think I was taking sides. They were as competitive about their health and fitness as they were about picking peas or playing Scrabble.

Addie had the last word this time. She'd picked up the flashlight from the hall table on our way out, and made a show of beaming it at Bea's feet as we walked under the oaks. The still air under the trees felt almost too thick to breathe.

"Feels like a storm's coming," Addie said, "Everything's holding its breath."

"We could use the rain. They aren't allowing campfires in the state parks." Bea looked straight ahead, ignoring her sister's efforts with the flashlight.

I was relieved when we got back to the open air of our lawn. My head felt jammed with thoughts too jumbled to talk about. "I think I'll go to bed and read," I said as we latched the door against a sudden swirl of wind.

"Don't you at least want a cold drink before you go up?" Addie was unhappy that I was missing bedtime snack as well as dinner, but I didn't think I could swallow anything even to please her.

I was halfway up the stairs when Bea called, "Did you find your letter? I put it on the dresser."

I made it to the top of the stairs and leaned against the wall. I closed my eyes and tried to take deep, slow breaths. Mama couldn't possibly know I'd been thinking about living in Heron Cove. Plus she'd only put Bea and Addie's names on the envelopes of the three short notes she'd written to us all.

The letter was from Grampa.

Dear Sage,

I broke down and cried when I saw those old sketches of mine. It's hard to believe Mother took them with her to Heron Cove and saved them all wrapped and labeled in her box. I can't get enough of looking at them, and of thinking about her taking such care.

As you can see, you've got me drawing again. This picture is how I remember you that time we were at the shore together.

My heart is with all of you there. I send my love and thanks.

Grampa

xo xo xo

Grampa had drawn a view of the field opening to the sea. At the edge of the water stood a little girl with wild, curly hair, her arms flung wide. Behind her, to one side, was Grampa, holding a small pair of sneakers in one hand.

I sat in the rocker, the letter and drawing on my lap, for a long time. Rain came suddenly in a thundering torrent. I could hear Bea and Addie shutting windows downstairs. I shut my own, then went down and gave the letter to Addie and the drawing to Bea.

"Welcome home, Elliot," Addie murmured after reading the note. She reached for an embroidered white handkerchief in her skirt pocket, and wiped her eyes.

Bea nodded, and cleared her throat. "I would guess Heron Cove is the home he always yearned for. Maybe now he will let himself claim it."

I had squeezed in between them on the sofa. "What about Spokane?" I asked. "He's lived there practically his whole life."

"And will continue to, I'm sure." Bea took my hand. "You don't have to give up one home to claim another."

I took a deep breath, and let it out slowly. The brass clock ticked from the hall bookcase. Bea and Addie's soft arms were warm against mine.

"Maybe I will have a little snack," I said. "I'm starved."

The air had cleared by the time I turned out my light.

A meteor streaked across the section of sky framed by my windows.

"You don't have to give up one home to claim another," Bea had said. That meant me, too. I didn't have to choose between Heron Cove and Hollins. Or between Bea and Addie and Mama. Not unless I wanted to.

It came to me then with the gentle sweetness of the fresh breeze: I didn't have to choose between my mother and my father, either.

There, alone in the dark with the sea's distant whisper, I felt a cold, hard place in me gone. I was left with a warm well of sadness for the father I would never know. And with a yearning for my mother so sudden and so intense I was out of bed searching frantically for my pad and pen to tell her . . .

What? Sitting cross-legged on my bed, pen ready, I hesitated. I knew with absolute certainty I wanted my mother. What I wasn't sure of, what I hadn't been sure of since she'd sent me away this summer, was whether she wanted me.

There it was. Underneath all my confusion about choosing between living in Heron Cove or Hollins was the terrible fear that maybe I wouldn't have any choice at all, that maybe Mama would decide it was better this way, her being on her own and me staying with Bea and Addie.

She'd made decisions like that before. "I loved him and

then I didn't," she'd said about my father. But he wasn't the only one she'd left behind. She'd pushed Gramma and Grampa away, and for no reason I could see, she'd stayed away from Bea and Addie. She'd dropped friends she'd once said she loved and plans she'd said were perfect for her.

I sat quietly and understood how scared I'd been, how scared I *was,* that Mama wanted to leave me behind, too. I remembered a dream I'd had when I was little, a dream where Mama had died. I'd taken the bread knife from the kitchen drawer, holding it against the edge of the counter so I could fall against its sharp point, because I knew I couldn't live without her.

That was no longer true. With this summer, I knew I could live without Mama. But I didn't want to. I very much did not want to.

I steadied my hand and wrote:

Dear Mama,
I was wondering if you are going to get me when
you are finished with your institute, or do you want
me to stay here longer? I like Heron Cove very
much, so that would be okay. But I want to come
home sometime. I can take the bus.

Your loving daughter forever,
Sage
xo

I tried not to wait for an answer to my letter. I knew Mama wasn't good about telephoning or writing. Most of the time I'd think how silly I was being, that of course my mother wanted me to come home, she was my *mother,* for heaven's sake. But then I'd remember how angry I'd been since my father died, and I wouldn't be so sure. Mama could probably tell when I was hating her. She might not want to be around someone like that.

One morning, Bea asked me to go to Beaverton with Mr. Weisner to do some errands. It would be just the two of us, and as soon as Bea asked, I knew there was something I wanted to talk to him about in private.

I waited until we were well past Ina Sims's store, then I turned toward him.

"My father died last winter," I said, though I was sure he knew that. "My mother never told him I was born. I was wondering, if you had a daughter, do you think you would want to know about her?

"I mean, if you and her mother had said good-bye before she was born?" I explained when he didn't answer right away.

Mr. Weisner looked at me in the nicest way. "I can't imagine not wanting to know you, Sage," he said. "But it would hardly be fair for me to second-guess your mother. I wasn't in her shoes."

"She thought he was a nice man," I said. "He was older than her, and he'd just gotten divorced." I took a big breath because I was feeling a little shaky. "She wanted to keep me, but not him."

Mr. Weisner drove for a bit, then said quietly, "I'm sure she did what she thought was best for you all, Sage. I'm also sure that if your father had known you, he would have loved you. If he was any kind of man at all, he would have loved you."

With him saying that, I knew it was true. I sat there and just felt it.

"One more thing," I said when we were getting near

Beaverton. "Do you think it would be okay with him if I found some of his family someday?"

Mr. Weisner hesitated. "Sage, I can only speak for myself. I think I would like that very much, and would hope my family would, too. But you'd have to prepare yourself for a variety of reactions. I'd hate to see you hurt."

I nodded. I'd seen shows on TV about people looking for lost families. "I was just wondering," I said.

"You will always wonder about your father." He said it gently, and I nodded again. Even if my father had the best family in the world, I still would never know him, and he'd never know me.

"If it would help any," Mr. Weisner said when we turned onto Main Street, "I would be honored to be your uncle Ben. Elizabeth and I have sadly missed having a girl in our family."

"Uncle Ben." I smiled at him. "Like the rice." I thought of what Bea had said my first day in Heron Cove. "We can't change what went before, but we can choose what to make of it."

"I'd like that," I said. "I'd like it a lot."

"Well then, this calls for a celebration." Mr. Weisner parked the car by the IGA and smiled his Santa smile at me. "You've made me an uncle, and a famous one at that."

"What kind of celebration?" I sounded so eager we both laughed.

"How about a picnic Friday night at Sheeps Head Point? The real thing. We'll build a fire and roast corn and hot dogs—"

"And s'mores," I said. "Let's have s'mores."

Mr. Weisner looked mystified. "That sounds like an exotic mushroom," he said. "Can we find them around here?"

I giggled. "It's a graham cracker, chocolate, toasted-marshmallow sandwich. It's so good you want some-more."

"Well then, we'd better buy the stuff here." He winked at me. "I wouldn't want Ina Sims to hear of this."

After the IGA, we went to the library and the bank. We were looking over a table of books outside the bookstore when a voice called, "Sage! Hey! Over here!"

I turned around and saw a girl waving frantically from the other side of the street. She was almost across before I recognized her. Her hair had grown in on the shaved side and was bright red now. She danced between the cars in the same purple high-top sneakers.

"Miriam!" I yelled, and ran to meet her. "What are you doing here?"

She gave me a hug. "I'm checking out the local color," she said with a grin. "What about you, kid? You look great!"

I pulled her back to the book table. "I'm doing errands with . . . my uncle Ben." I took his hand and said, "This is my friend Miriam. I met her on the bus."

"Hello, Miriam." Mr. Weisner shook her hand. He just had the kindest blue eyes as he looked at her.

"Hello," she said. I could see her noticing. "I didn't know Sage had an uncle here, too."

"Newly found," he said. "We're about to get some lunch. Would you like to join us?"

"Thanks, but I'm here with some guys from work. We've got to get back." Miriam looked at me and smiled. "I'm glad I saw you, kid. You had me worried. You looked lost that day."

I smiled back. "So did you."

"Things are working out," Miriam said. "My mother left my father. I think she means it this time. She moved into an apartment just big enough for her and me. I'm going back after Labor Day and finish school." She rummaged in her pack. "Let's keep in touch. You tell me your stories, I'll tell you mine. Two heads, you know . . ." She scribbled an address and phone number on the back of a sales slip, then tore off a piece for me to use. I wrote down both Heron Cove and Hollins, just in case.

I tucked her paper carefully into the button pocket of my shirt. Even with all my worry about Mama, my world had never felt bigger.

*F*riday was a warm wild day of sun one minute and downpours the next. The wind sent Bea's watering can banging off the steps way across into the field. I was worried our picnic plans would be ruined, but in late afternoon the sky cleared enough for everybody to agree to give it a try.

After Irene Perry came to care for any bed-and-breakfast guests who might show up, we drove out along the bumpy track by Sims's store that led to Sheeps Head Point. The Weisners were unloading their car as Addie braked to a lurching stop.

"We'll have to stay back a bit," Uncle Ben shouted. "There's a buster of a storm at sea."

I'd never seen anything like it. The whole ocean rolled and heaved. It surged toward shore, burst on the rocks, and exploded skyward.

We found a level place back from the spray where we spread an old shower curtain. Addie made a circle of rocks and got a fire going with pinecones and driftwood the Weisners had brought.

"There!" she said as the flickering flames strengthened to a blaze. "I do have a way with fires."

The adults settled into beach chairs. "You kids go find some puddles of seawater and soak the corn," Uncle Ben said. "And stay back from the edge. A rogue wave could sweep you clear around to Halifax before you knew what hit you."

Jamie was unusually quiet as we dragged the sack of corn between us over the rocks. We upended the bag with a splash into a crevice the size of a bathtub full of salt water.

"So," Jamie said as we prodded the bobbing ears with the toes of our sneakers. "When's your mother coming?"

I shook my head and shrugged. "I haven't heard yet. Her school ends next week, but I don't know if she's coming then."

"Really?" Jamie brightened. "You might stay longer?"

"Maybe." I started stuffing the dripping corn back into the sack. "Come on. I'm starved."

Uncle Ben cooked the corn in the coals of the fire. It was the best I ever tasted. We roasted hot dogs on sticks and had potato salad made from Bea's new potatoes. Then we toasted marshmallows and squashed them between graham crackers and Hershey bars until the chocolate was all gooey. I ate four, even more than Jamie.

"Food for royalty," Aunt Elizabeth said as she licked her sticky fingers. "Great idea, this picnic. The summer was getting away from me." She rinsed her hands with leftover tea. "Come sit by me, Sage honey, and let me play with your hair. I've been dying to get my hands in it all summer. Now that I'm your aunt . . ."

I leaned against her knees while she stroked and arranged my hair. Uncle Ben and Addie took turns telling stories as a canopy of clouds drew an early dark around the circle of our fire.

I was roused from my bliss by a poke from Jamie. "Look! A light!" He pointed down the shore, but I couldn't see anything. Then a tiny light flickered way along the point and was gone.

"Let's check it out!" Jamie leaped to his feet, dragging me with him. We stopped outside the firelight to let our eyes adjust, and saw the light again.

"They must have come out on the old backshore road." Jamie spoke directly into my ear, as though anyone could hear us above the roar of the sea.

We went as fast as we dared over the wet rocks. Jamie shushed me sternly every time I giggled.

"There it is!" He grabbed my arm as a light flashed not far ahead of us. I could make out the dark outline of something that seemed to expand and contract as it moved slowly along.

"It's two people," I whispered. "They're probably out to see the waves."

"Way down here? In this dark?" Jamie was moving closer, pulling me with him.

"Let's go back," I said, resisting. "Maybe they want to be alone."

"That's just it!" Jamie hissed in my ear. "I think we should see what they're up to. There's a history of smugglers along this coast, renegades who'd stop at nothing to protect their profits."

"And you want to introduce yourself?" I felt a thrill of apprehension there in the dark so far from the others.

"I just want to get close enough to see what they're doing." Jamie continued to pick his way cautiously over the rocks toward the light that danced around the looming shadow. I followed, bent low, torn between giggles and terror.

I rammed headfirst into him when he stopped without warning. We clutched each other to keep from falling as the couple ahead turned. Their flashlight briefly lit the face of Ina Sims. She was looking up at the man with her. She was laughing, though we couldn't hear it above the noise of the sea.

"Oh my," I whispered. "Ina Sims is out with a beau."

"I never even saw her *smile*." Jamie seemed more surprised than if we'd actually found smugglers.

I tugged at him. "Let's get out of here. They're coming back."

"Who do you suppose she's with?" I asked when we were at a safe distance.

Jamie shook his head. "I couldn't see, and I can't even guess. I never saw her with anybody around Heron Cove."

"Well," I said in my best Ina Sims voice, "*I* think they could use a little supervision."

Only a few coals were left of the fire, and the adults were starting to pack up by the time we got back.

"It was Ina Sims!" Jamie announced.

"With a man!" I flopped down into a beach chair.

"What man?" Bea asked.

"What were they doing?" Addie dropped the shower curtain she was folding.

"That," I said, "is what *we'd* like to know."

"Was he tall or short? Fat or thin?" Aunt Elizabeth asked.

"I couldn't tell about the fat part," Jamie said. "But he was quite a bit taller than she was."

"That lets out Roy Fowler, then." Bea opened up the chair she was holding and sat down again. The others did the same.

"Roy Fowler never looked at a woman in his life, Bea," Addie said.

"I know that, Addie, but who else is there in Heron Cove?"

"He doesn't have to be from around here, does he?" I could tell Uncle Ben was enjoying the game. He leaned forward, and whispered dramatically, "He doesn't even have to be available."

"Well," Addie said, considering, "Ina's in the store seven days a week. I don't know how she'd meet somebody from any distance. As for available . . ." She shook her head. "No, not Ina Sims."

"Does she have a brother?" I asked, though I didn't think that shadow had looked like a brother and sister.

"Walter's in California, she doesn't get along with Floyd, and Burr was killed in the war," Bea said. She added primly, "Not that it's any of our business."

"Of course it's not," Addie agreed, "though we're hardly discussing it with everyone who comes in for their milk or their mail."

"That's true," Bea said. "I guess Ina's own tongue does offer the green light on this." Having decided that, she helped us come up with increasingly ridiculous ideas of who the man with Ina Sims was.

"I like the theory about the IRS agent," Jamie said later as he and I lugged the cooler to his car. "I've read that small businesses are having to deal with more and more regulations. Maybe Ina missed some or messed up. It happens all the time. So say she's faced with losing the store, so she tries to strike a deal—"

"At Sheeps Head Point?"

"Well, if he doesn't go along with it, she can push him in the surf. He wouldn't stand a chance on a night like this. She could always say he slipped."

"Ina Sims isn't a murderer," I said, jabbing his shoulder with my free hand.

"That's what the neighbors always say about murderers." Jamie waggled his eyebrows at me as he climbed in behind his parents.

We bumped slowly along the rutted road, calling last good nights when we reached the pavement.

"A rousing good time," Addie said as she turned into our drive.

Ahead of us, parked by the kitchen door, was a small red car with Massachusetts license plates.

$\mathcal{G}$ood thing we asked Irene to tend shop," Bea said at the sight of the out-of-state car. "Do we have enough bacon for breakfast, Addie?"

Little thrills shivered through me as I took the picnic basket from the trunk. I hurried to the door, then hung back until Addie reached around me for the latch.

Mama was laughing and drinking tea at the kitchen table with Irene Perry.

I couldn't seem to move. With cries of welcome and exclamations of surprise, Bea and Addie prodded me forward. Irene Perry beamed as though she'd planned this all along.

"Look at you!" Mama hugged me, held me off at

arm's length, then hugged me again. Her eyes were shiny with tears. "You must have grown an inch a week! Just look at you!"

I felt numb with confusion. The institute wasn't over yet, was it? Whose car was that? I saw Mama check out my hair. I knew it was wild from the wind after Aunt Elizabeth had unbraided it. Mama liked my hair to be tied down.

"Where did you get the car?" I blurted. "Why are you here?"

Mama laughed. "I wanted to see you," she said. "And the car is ours. I decided it was time to invest in something more reliable."

Bea drove Irene Perry home while Addie put away the picnic stuff. I helped Mama take her things up to the guest room. I still felt tongue-tied, but she didn't seem to notice. I could tell she was in one of her all's-right-with-the-world moods.

Later I sat on the sofa between Mama and Addie. I watched Bea's needle wink in and out of her quilt squares as they talked about this and that like friendly strangers. After a while I said I was tired, and kissed them all good night.

"*Good* night, my darling." Mama held my face between her hands when she kissed me. "I'll look in when I come up."

Instead of going upstairs, I went out the front door. The sky had cleared and the moon was bright, but the surf still crashed on the shore. I skirted Mama's car as though it were a strange dog and went across the damp lawn.

The path to the sea was a dark ribbon in the moonlit field. I headed for the cormorant rock at the end of the beach. Water foamed near my feet, misting me with spray. I sat with my chin on my knees and watched the moonlight flow and shatter with the waves. Slowly my confusion cleared. Mama was here, obviously happy to see me, as well as Bea and Addie. That was enough for now.

I stood up and stretched, my arms open wide, my hair billowing back like a sail. A scream ripped through the noise of the surf. Whirling, I lost my balance and fell. The scream came again, this time in the shape of my name. "Sage! Sage!"

I picked myself up out of the puddles left by the re-treating sea.

"Oh my God! Oh my God! Don't you ever do that again!" My mother grabbed my sleeve and dragged me back up the beach.

"Mama!" I wrenched my arm free. "What's the matter with you?"

"With *me*? What's the matter with *me*?" Mama

sucked in a deep, trembling breath. "I went to your room and you weren't there. Bea and Addie didn't seem at all concerned. They said check the shore. I almost broke my ankle on that path, and then when I heard the surf . . ." Mama inhaled again. "You stood up on that rock like you were going to . . . you *disappeared* . . . those waves . . ."

"The waves weren't near the rock, Mama. I fell on the beach." I smothered an urge to laugh. Wet sand was clumped down the back of me, and Mama looked plain crazy. Her eyes were like saucers, and wisps of her hair stood up in the wind like antennae.

"I thought I'd lost you." Mama slumped down onto a driftwood log and began to cry. I sat beside her and patted her shoulder.

After a long while, Mama said more calmly, "That letter you wrote, Sage. You sounded like you weren't sure you'd be coming home again, like maybe I'd *abandoned* you."

She took my hand that was still patting her shoulder and held it in both of hers. "I want to tell you, Sage . . ." She paused, and I leaned in close so I could hear better. "A woman named Inga Schuler ran the herb institute. She spoke with a heavy German accent. She stopped me after lunch one day, just before I got your letter, and she said, 'I notice you, Andrea, becoming disillusioned with us here. You turn away, we cannot go forward together.'

I didn't much like her, and I was angry she spoke to me like that. Then your letter came."

Mama sighed deeply. "I sat with that letter for the longest time. It occurred to me that maybe Inga Schuler was right. Maybe I *was* turning away. From you. And that was the one thing I swore I'd never do to a child of mine. I was horrified. I didn't want to think it was so. I wanted to blame everyone else, even you."

I stayed perfectly still.

Mama kissed my hand and said, "I was about your age when things began to go bad between me and my parents. I was cute and well behaved as a small child. My mother loved to dress me and show me off. But I didn't stay cute. My teeth came in crowded, my hair was impossible. In sixth grade I was bigger than all the boys in my dance class.

"My mother fussed at me like she was trying to salvage a cake that fell apart coming out of the pan. Nothing about me pleased her. My hatred of her became the one thing I felt good about."

"What about Grampa?" I asked.

"He wouldn't take sides," Mama said. "He wouldn't speak up for me. He'd just sit there looking helpless when she'd say some mean thing. I hated my mother, but I felt betrayed by my father.

"I tried to make life as miserable for them as they were making it for me. When I was fourteen, they'd had enough of me and sent me away to a school whose main subject was discipline. My father did try to convince my mother to let me go to Bea or Addie, but in the end he gave in on that, too."

"Bea and Addie told me," I said.

"At least I didn't repeat *that* mistake," Mama said. "I may have sent you away this summer, Sage, but I sent you here. And at the time, I didn't see it as sending you away. Certainly not for long."

"Then you were planning to come and get me?" I asked. "All along?"

Mama put her arm around me. "Of *course* I was planning to get you, you mean everything in the *world* to me. I just thought we might do well to be apart for a while. You know as well as I do that things have been difficult between us lately. I guess I was hurt, I didn't understand. . . ." Mama was still for a minute. Then she said in a level voice, "I was frightened, Sage. I was scared of losing you. And the truth is, I'd rather walk away than have you push me away."

I remembered how Mama used to say, with a smile and a hug, "It's you and me against the world, Sage." She could probably tell, as I got older, that wasn't enough for me. This summer had felt like coming out of a narrow maze into open air. It had never occurred to me that Mama might feel left behind.

I couldn't stop myself. "Is that why you left Robert? So he wouldn't have the chance to leave you?"

I felt Mama stiffen. "I don't know. I didn't think of it that way at the time. We parted good friends."

"He was my *father*!"

My mother took her arm from around me. "I know that perfectly well, Sage. But certainly not in any emotional sense. You never knew him."

"How can you *say* that?" I wailed. "I thought about him all the *time*! I pretended about his *family*. I was going to *find* him, and now it's *too late*! He never even *knew* about me! He . . . never . . . knew!" I was yelling at her. I was howling.

My mother's silence echoed.

What had I done? Why had I said that?

And then her arms came back around me. "Sage!" she said, rocking me. "It's all right! I'm sorry! I didn't know! Oh God, I'm sorry, I'm so sorry!

"Please help me, Sage," Mama said when my sobs had quieted. "I had no idea how you felt. I didn't want to tie your father to our lives after he and I went our separate ways. You were mine, only mine. That was all I wanted, all I thought you would want. When Mrs. Ashford told me you were grieving, I didn't believe her. Maybe I just didn't want to, I hardly know."

When I didn't say anything, Mama hugged me hard. "Please, Sage! I do want to know. I'll try to understand, if you just tell me."

I nodded. I felt very tired. There were some things that couldn't really be explained. Mama could try to understand, but it wasn't the same as her knowing from her own heart.

Mama wiped my cheeks and held the tissue for me to blow my nose, the way she used to when I was little. We were together again. That's what mattered right now.

I see you have guests," Ina Sims said before I was through the screen door of the store the next morning. I'd come early, hoping to get there before Irene Perry told her about Mama.

"Yes," was all I said. "Is the mail in yet? And Addie wants two pounds of Cabot Cheddar."

"Personal or paying?" Ina asked as she sliced through the wheel of cheese.

I pretended not to understand.

"Your *guests!*" Ina said, her frustration starting to show. "Do you know them, or are they bed-and-breakfast?"

"Oh!" I nodded. "It's someone we know."

Ina stared at me, waiting.

"That was quite a storm at sea last night, wasn't it?" I said.

Her lips tightened. "So I hear."

"We were picnicking at Sheeps Head Point," I went on. "I'd never seen the ocean like that."

Ina turned to the mail. "Looks like you got another letter from Elliot," she said. "I should think Bea and Addie would appreciate a little of the attention he lavishes on you."

"We were wondering who the man was," I said.

Ina stopped shuffling the letters. "What man?" she asked, without looking at me.

"The man you were with at Sheeps Head Point," I said. "None of us could figure out who he was."

Ina's hands started moving again, but they were shaking. "Just a friend," she said. Red spots flared on her cheeks. "An old friend who happens to like watching storms at sea." She studied a flyer from Barney's Discount Beverages. "I met him years ago when I was at secretary school in Bangor."

I thought she was going to tell me more, and she did.

"We were engaged to be married."

She glanced at me, but I didn't even blink. "We were all set to elope before he left for Korea, but I detected the smell of alcohol on him and broke it off. I hadn't seen him in years, then there he was doing a hooked-rug demonstration of all things at the Beaverton Craft Fair." The corners of her mouth twitched. "He was real pleased to see me, treated me to some cider, and asked if he could call. . . ."

Her eyes snapped up and nailed me. "Don't you go making anything of this, now. We've been nothing but proper. I don't hold with entertaining single men in my home, and William respects that."

"I'm glad you found each other again," I said.

Ina Sims looked startled. "Yes," she said. "Well. Thank you. Maybe it's time people know we're seeing each other. Better fact than fiction. As I've never been one for gossip, I trust people will accord me some of that same respect now."

She rang up the cheese briskly. "Your guests are from Massachusetts?" she asked. She'd obviously seen or heard about the license plate.

I was happy to satisfy her. "It's Mama," I said. "We're together again, too."

"Well, I'm pleased to hear that. There's entirely too much everybody going their own way these days without a thought for family obligations." Ina's voice followed me out the door. "You tell Andrea to stop by and say hello before she hightails it out of here. I probably won't recognize her, it's been that long."

Bea and Addie were most satisfyingly amazed when I told them about Ina's William.

"Doesn't surprise me in the least," Addie declared, after she'd exclaimed in astonishment throughout the entire telling.

Mama hadn't been listening. She was reading the letter I got from Grampa. He'd sent a drawing of his cat, Ginger, looking out from under a tomato plant in his garden. He said he wanted to come to Heron Cove next summer. He hoped I would be there, too. He said if Gramma didn't feel up to the trip, he'd find someone to come in and stay with her.

"He's always had a cat," Mama said. "And a garden. My mother doesn't like his attention to either, but he's always had them anyway."

I wanted to tell her what I'd learned about Grampa, about what happened when he was young, and about the drawings we'd found and sent to him. I wanted to show her his letters and tell her how good he'd been with me on the beach when I was six.

She'd said she would listen. She'd said she would try to understand. Maybe that meant about her father as well as mine.

I went and leaned against her. "Let's walk up to the cemetery," I said. "I want to show you what I planted."

*W*e sat by the family stones in the cemetery, just like Bea and I did my first day in Heron Cove. I told Mama about Grampa's parents, Anna McClure and Lorenzo Miller. I told her about Charlie dying, about Anna coming back to Heron Cove with Bea and Addie, about Grampa being left alone to work the farm with his father. Mama knew some of what happened, but not why. When I told her about the drawings, she cried.

Addie was taking blueberry pies from the oven when we got back. "Is there anything you'd especially like to do while you're here, Andrea?" she asked my mother.

"I'd like to go to Lexfield," Mama said.

"Lexfield!" For a moment Addie looked like Mama had suggested we take off for Mars. She set the last pie carefully on the counter and said, "Well, I guess that's easy enough. We can go this afternoon."

"I can't think when we were there last," Bea said. "We just don't seem to go in that direction."

"I could find my way," Mama said. "You may not care to—"

"Nonsense!" Addie interrupted briskly. "It would be hard to explain just where the farm was. The house and barn burned years ago, you know. And we really should check on things at the cemetery there."

"I wonder if blueberries still grow in the upper field," Bea said. "We'll take a pail. The knoll used to be covered, remember, Addie?"

"We'd fill the kettle and Mother would act like we'd brought her the crown jewels." Addie smiled. "The thought of her pleasure kept me picking. You took to things like that even then, Bea. I just wanted to sit in the shade."

"You were a lazy one," Bea agreed. "I was always terrified Pa was going to get after you."

"I don't think *lazy* is the word," Addie said stiffly while Bea winked at me behind her back. "I just had different interests."

We set out in Mama's new car as soon as we'd cleaned

up after lunch. Addie sat in the backseat with me and issued instructions. The afternoon heat intensified when we turned away from the sea onto the Lexfield road. It shimmered off the ribbon of tar that stretched through miles of scrub. Bea said in winter the wind across those barrens made snowdrifts that used to cut Lexfield off from Heron Cove for months at a time.

Lexfield, she told us as we got near, had once been a fair-size town. But when fire destroyed the church and the school, the community died out, too. Now it was just a crossroads marked by a store with two gas pumps. Houses and trailers were scattered here and there with no sense of connection.

The Miller farm was almost two miles beyond the store. The house had been on one side of the road and the barn on the other. We found parts of the stone foundation of the barn. I picked up a rusted iron spike, and a buckle Bea said was from a harness. A dried-up well under a gnarled apple tree and a corner of cellar stones were the only things left to show where the house had been.

We walked along the dirt road and turned up a hill still covered with blueberry bushes. Bea and I picked nearly a quart on the way up while Mama and Addie pushed through the thickets straight to the top. They were sitting on soft moss, enjoying the view, when we reached them.

Far across the barrens, the sea glistened on the horizon. "Mother used to come up here every chance she got," Bea said. "She'd show us right where Heron Cove was." On the other side of the ridge, she said, was where her father and brothers had been cutting wood the day Charlie died.

I was thinking about Charlie walking along that road through the snow as we went back to the car. My great-grandmother Anna must have followed her sons to the cemetery on the same road we drove back to the crossroads. Bea and Addie were quiet. I was worried they were feeling sad, but they seemed to enjoy visiting with the owner when we stopped at the store for ice cream.

The cemetery was next to where the church had been. Lorenzo Miller's grave was near the back corner by a stone wall. Bea had brought clippers, and though the dry brown grass was neatly trimmed, she clipped carefully all around her father's flat gray stone. Addie sat fanning herself on the wall while Mama copied dates and inscriptions in her pocket notebook.

There were other Miller stones, but I thought Lorenzo's looked lonely off to the side by the wall. I felt in my pocket for some of the lupine seedpods I'd picked in the field at Heron Cove to take home to Hollins. When Bea was finished with the clippers, I used them to break through the dry, dense turf by my great-grandfather's grave. I speared and pried until I'd cleared a small patch of gold-colored earth. I pushed the seeds into the crumbly soil and patted it smooth.

"Amen," Bea said when I finished.

"Indeed," Addie said.

For as long as I could remember, Mama had carried a tiny carved ivory mask on her key chain. Now she carefully worked it off the spiraled ring and tucked it into the soil along with the seeds.

$\mathcal{M}$ama had planned to stay just that weekend, but one day led to another until it was a whole week before we started back to Hollins. Every day, protected from the sun with a big hat and long sleeves and pants, she went across the field with me to see what the tide had washed up. We picnicked with the Weisners by the creek behind their house, and at Sheeps Head Point. We went back to Lexfield to pick more blueberries, and we helped can them for winter pies.

Ina Sims's William had been seen in town, and everybody was talking about it. Bea and Addie began planning their contributions to the church fair, which was held every year on the last Saturday of September.

"I wish I could be here for it," I said. "People come from all over."

"I know," Mama said. "But it will be good to get back to Hollins, too, Sage. Maybe we can invite the Swanes to dinner. They've been a second family to you since kindergarten."

I stopped at every house between ours and the store to say good-bye.

"Go on with you, now," Ed Perry said when I gave him a hug. He promised to write me if he remembered any more stories.

Irene Perry gave me a lavender sachet for my underwear drawer, and Lena Osborne gave me a plate with a picture of the church painted on it.

"It's left over from a fund-raiser we had a couple years back," she said. "I thought you might like to have it."

We planned to leave early on Saturday morning. When I came down to breakfast, Jamie was already at the table, eating the peach pancakes Addie had made for our good-bye.

"What are you doing here?" I asked as I sat down across from him.

"I got up early to mow the churchyard," he said. "It's the last time I do it before we go back to Orono."

"It's barely light out!" I said. "The dew won't dry off for hours!"

Jamie was concentrating on his plate. "Well, the thing is . . ." He brightened suddenly. "Do you have a bird feeder in Hollins?"

"Yes," I said cautiously. "I fill it every day, except for when I was here."

"Do you have evening grosbeaks in winter? Pine grosbeaks? How about blue jays?"

"Sometimes," I said. "Not as many as we used to have." I swiped up syrup with a wedge of cheese. "Why?"

"Because"—Jamie stared across at me intently— "we've seen the same decline here! I know blue jays had a throat parasite a while back, habitats keep changing . . . I'm going to get more information, but I thought if we both kept records. . . ."

I looked straight back at him and laughed. "I'll write you, Jamie. And I'll be back. Every summer. It's all decided."

Mama wouldn't make any promises about coming with me. "I feel like we're arranging visitation rights," she'd said when we talked about it with Bea and Addie. Her mouth had smiled, but her eyes were sad.

"My dear Andrea." Bea had taken Mama's hand in both of hers. "Our joy would be complete if you let Heron Cove be your home, too."

"I know," Mama said. "I know."

Bea and Addie were waiting for me at the edge of

the field when I returned from one last good-bye to the shore.

"We want you to have this, dear," Addie said. She folded my hand around a velvet drawstring bag.

Inside was the gold ring we'd seen in Anna's box the day we found Grampa's drawings.

"We had it enlarged," Bea said. "Grandfather brought this back from one of his voyages when Mother was just six years old. She was the apple of his eye."

Mama had the car packed and running. With the gold ring shining on my middle finger, I waved all the way through the tunnel of oaks, past the cemetery, past the store, where I flung a kiss to Ina Sims, who was waving from the door.